S
2013

BULLETS DON'T DIE

Center Point
Large Print

Also by J. A. Johnstone and available from Center Point Large Print:

Rattlesnake Valley
Trail of Blood
Killer Poker
Blood of Renegades
Crossfire
Inferno
Brutal Vengeance
Hard Luck Money

Also by William W. Johnstone with J. A. Johnstone:

The Butcher of Bear Creek
Massacre Canyon
Hard Ride to Hell
Those Jensen Boys!

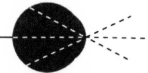

**This Large Print Book carries the
Seal of Approval of N.A.V.H.**

THE LONER:

BULLETS DON'T DIE

J. A. Johnstone

CENTER POINT LARGE PRINT
THORNDIKE, MAINE

This Center Point Large Print edition is published in the year 2016 by arrangement with Kensington Publishing Corp.

The text of this Large Print edition is unabridged. In other aspects, this book may vary from the original edition. Printed in the United States of America on permanent paper. Set in 16-point Times New Roman type.

ISBN: 978-1-62899-873-3

Library of Congress Cataloging-in-Publication Data

Names: Johnstone, J. A., author.
Title: Bullets don't die : the loner / J. A. Johnstone.
Other titles: Bullets do not die
Description: Center Point Large Print edition. | Thorndike, Maine : Center Point Large Print, 2016. | ©2012
Identifiers: LCCN 2015043314 | ISBN 9781628998733
  (hardcover : alk. paper)
Subjects: LCSH: Large type books. | GSAFD: Western stories.
Classification: LCC PS3610.O43 B85 2016 | DDC 813/.6—dc23
LC record available at http://lccn.loc.gov/2015043314

BULLETS
DON'T DIE

Chapter 1

Texas was a long way behind him now, and with it the dangers he had faced while carrying out an undercover assignment for a friend of his in the Texas Rangers.

For the last few years, the man known as Kid Morgan had spent most of his time wandering the southwestern states and territories. True, he had crossed the country once during that time, going to Boston and from there all the way west to San Francisco, but at that time he had been involved in a quest that ultimately proved to be futile.

He didn't like to think about that anymore.

From Texas he had drifted north, through the territory of Oklahoma and on into Kansas, veering slightly west of north and heading away from the endless plains devoted to farming in the eastern part of the state.

Some good-sized ranches were out there, The Kid had heard, and he was toying with the idea of becoming a cowboy.

Why not? he had asked himself when that thought came to mind. A few years earlier, he had decided he was going to be a gunfighter, hadn't he? Millionaire businessman Conrad Browning had disappeared, and Kid Morgan, the Scourge of the Plains, the Pistoleer from Nowhere, the

Deadly Shootist with the Tragic Past, had been born.

The thing of it was, he *did* have a tragic past, and his new identity as Kid Morgan had been designed to help him gain revenge on the men responsible. He had quickly discovered it wasn't just a pose, either. From his father, the notorious gunfighter Frank Morgan, he had inherited the speed, the coordination between hand and eye, and the cool nerves under fire that allowed him to be a dangerous gunman in his own right.

Kid Morgan had begun as fiction, but now he was fact.

That was fine with The Kid. Nothing was drawing him back to his old life as Conrad Browning.

So if he wanted to be a cowboy, indeed, why not?

There was, however, one distinction between the two situations. He had possessed the skills he needed to survive as a gunfighter. Other than being a good rider, he had no idea if he could handle the job of working on a ranch.

There was only one way to find out, he'd told himself, and so he rode aimlessly across the prairies of western Kansas, looking for a suitable spread where he could ask for a job.

The terrain was low, rolling hills, virtually treeless except for the places where a creek twisted its way across the landscape. The banks of those creeks were often lined with small cotton-woods.

The Kid spotted a line of those trees in the distance during the late afternoon and pointed his buckskin toward them, leading his pack horse. He could probably push on for another hour or so, he thought, but what reason did he have to do that? The creek up ahead would provide a good place to camp, and he was going to take advantage of it.

He was still a couple hundred yards from the trees when he heard a single gunshot. The pistol's roar was repeated in diminishing echoes rolling away across the hills.

The Kid reined in. He didn't think the shot had been directed at him, but still gave some thought to circling wide around the spot. He wasn't looking for trouble.

A pistol shot didn't always mean trouble. Somebody could have shot a snake. It was possible the person was hurt and was trying to attract attention, although three evenly spaced shots was the accepted frontier signal for a plea for help.

Mostly, though, Kid Morgan wasn't the sort of hombre who rode *around* anything. He hitched the buckskin into motion again and headed for the creek.

If trouble was waiting for him, he was well armed to meet it. A holstered Colt .45 rode on his hip, and in his right-hand saddlebag, within easy reach, was a semiautomatic Mauser C96 pistol, fully loaded with a ten-round clip. He had carried the German-made weapon for a while, but recently switched back to the old reliable Colt. The broom handle Mauser made a mighty fine second gun, though.

In addition, the butt of a Winchester Model 1894 carbine in .30-30 caliber stuck up from a saddle boot on the left side of the horse. The Kid had an old Sharps buffalo rifle strapped to his pack horse for long-distance shooting.

And if there was close work that needed to be done, a razor-sharp Bowie knife was sheathed on his left hip.

Some people might have said he was armed for bear, but The Kid wasn't really worried about bears, especially on the Kansas prairie.

Men, on the other hand . . .

As he drew closer to the creek, he was able to see several figures moving around on the near bank. A couple men moved to the edge of the trees and watched him approach.

He lifted a hand in greeting and to show he was peaceful. He counted four men, but only three mounts were visible. That didn't bode well, especially considering the single shot he'd heard.

The Kid reined to a halt about twenty feet from the two men keeping an eye on him. One was painfully skinny, dressed in a threadbare town suit, a collarless shirt with no tie, and a battered old derby. The other was shorter and stockier, with a close-cropped dark beard peppered with silver. He spoke, nodding to The Kid. "Howdy, mister."

"Are you fellas planning on camping here?" The Kid asked. "Because I don't want to intrude."

"No, we just stopped to water our horses and let 'em rest for a spell." The stocky man thumbed back the black Stetson he wore. "Too bad, though. My pard Jeff's horse couldn't make it. Poor critter was plumb worn out. Jeff had to shoot it. It was hard on him, too. He'd had that horse for a long time."

"Yeah," one of the men standing by the edge of the creek called. "Hate to lose that animal, but there wasn't nothin' else to do."

The Kid could see the dark shape of the dead horse on the ground beside the man. "Sorry," he acknowledged, without feeling much real sympathy. The three horses still standing were covered with drying sweat lather. Their heads hung low, and their sides were heaving. They hadn't been there long.

Men didn't come so close to killing their horses —by running them into the ground—unless they were in an awful big hurry. And men in that big a hurry usually had trouble hard on their heels.

The Kid kept his face expressionless and didn't let on that he understood that. Maybe he could still ride away without any gunplay, but he doubted it. He lifted the buckskin's reins with his left hand. "I guess I'll be moving along. Hope your luck takes a turn for the better."

"Oh, I reckon it already did." The stocky man tried to look like he wasn't doing anything, but his hand moved closer to the gun on his hip. "Our luck changed when you came along, mister. You've got two good horses there, one to replace Jeff's and one for a spare for the rest of us."

"Yeah," The Kid said, "but they're *my* horses."

The stocky man dropped the act. His hand flashed to his gun. Next to him, the skinny man in the derby clawed at a Smith & Wesson he wore in a cross-draw rig. Back in the trees, the other two men slapped leather as they split up and spread out.

The Kid took care of the problem right in front of him first. He palmed the Colt from its holster and fired, sending the bullet into the middle of the stocky man's chest, which was admittedly a pretty good-sized target. The man had barely cleared leather and hadn't gotten off a shot.

The buckskin was accustomed to the roar of shots, but even so the horse moved a short distance to the left. The Kid took advantage of that, lining himself up for a better shot at the derby-wearing gent.

The man in the derby triggered the Smith & Wesson, and it cracked wickedly. The shot was pretty accurate, coming close enough The Kid felt the pulse of the slug passing through the air near his ear.

An instant later his second shot ripped through the skinny man's body, spinning him around and knocking him off his feet.

Dealing with the other two was going to be trickier. They had gone in opposite directions and had the cottonwoods to use as cover. Muzzle flashes stabbed at The Kid from both directions. He had to choose, so he swung his Colt to the right.

Something struck him in the chest with stunning impact from the left. He felt himself falling and knew he was sliding from the saddle. He kicked his feet free of the stirrups and smashed into the ground, stunned and helpless.

Chapter 2

The sensation lasted only a second or two. As a bullet kicked up dirt a couple feet away from him, The Kid recovered enough to roll toward the trees. The slender trunks of the cottonwoods wouldn't provide much cover, but they were better than nothing.

Bullets continued to zip and whine through the air and thud into the ground around him, kicking up sprays of dirt. He came to a stop next to one of the trees and tried to make himself as small as he could behind it.

His Colt was still in his hand—instinct had made him hang on to it—so he thrust the revolver around the cottonwood and triggered a shot toward the man on his right, who was also using the trees for cover.

He couldn't see the man on his left anymore, the one who had shot him, and that worried him.

Some men who lived by the gun preached the philosophy you had to believe you were invincible, that there was no gunfight you wouldn't win, no bullet that could kill you. The Kid's somewhat fatalistic nature, which dated back to before he had taken up the gun himself, made it impossible for him to adopt that attitude.

Still, he was surprised he'd been wounded. The men had the look of low-level hardcases, the sort who robbed general stores instead of holding up banks and trains, and he had figured his speed and accuracy would be enough to take care of all of them.

Clearly, he had underestimated at least one of them.

A slug chewed bark off the trunk above his head. The Kid snapped a return shot to the right and was rewarded by a grunt of pain. He had scored a hit, but it wasn't enough to put his opponent out of the fight. The man continued to fire at him.

As The Kid ducked his head, he tried to take stock of how badly he was hurt. The upper left part of his chest, as well as the shoulder and arm on that side of his body, were numb. It wasn't uncommon when a bullet first struck, but the wound should be starting to hurt, he thought.

He laid the Colt on the ground and reached over to explore the injury. He expected to feel the warm, wet stickiness of fresh blood, but all he found was a ragged rip in his shirt. Underneath it was the round, waterproof metal container he used to carry matches.

A grim smile tugged at the corners of The Kid's mouth. The bullet had come in at a very shallow angle, struck the metal cylinder, and glanced off rather than penetrating. The impact had been enough to knock him out of the saddle and make his arm and shoulder go numb. A couple inches either way and he would probably be dead.

The Kid had long since learned to accept the utter capriciousness of fate.

He also knew enough not to turn down good luck whenever he got it.

Knowing he wasn't going to bleed to death made him feel better, but he was still in a bad spot. He was caught in a crossfire . . . or at least he would have been if the fellow on the left was still shooting.

The man's gun had gone quiet. The Kid hadn't sent a shot in that direction, so he knew he hadn't killed the man. He figured the hombre was up to something.

15

The Kid kept glancing back and forth, hoping to catch a glimpse of his enemy working his way around to a better angle. The creek twisted in his direction, making it easy for the man to slip along the stream using the bank as cover until he was practically behind—

The Kid's thoughts stopped abruptly as the realization made him roll in that direction just as the man stood up from behind the creek bank and pointed a rifle at him. The Kid brought his Colt around to try for a shot of his own, but knew he was probably too late. He might as well be a target in a shooting gallery.

"Hey!"

The unexpected shout made the rifleman hesitate. He turned his head to look to his right just as a shot blasted.

The Kid saw the man's head jerk, saw the bright pink spray of blood, bone, and brain matter explode from the back of his skull. Somebody had drilled him right through the head.

As the rifleman collapsed, dropping out of sight, thudding footsteps warned The Kid the last gunman was charging him, trying to take advantage of the fact that The Kid had turned his back for a moment.

The Kid twisted around again. A bullet smacked into the ground and sprayed dirt in his eyes. He winced as he was momentarily blinded.

But he had already spotted the man running

through the trees toward him, and he let his instincts guide his shots as he tipped up the Colt's barrel and triggered twice.

As he blinked rapidly, trying to clear his vision, he heard the final man cry out. The shooting stopped.

When he was once again able to see, The Kid realized the man had dropped his gun and had both hands pressed to his belly. Blood welled between his fingers. He groaned, and then his eyes rolled up in their sockets. He went down like a puppet with its strings cut. Gutshot like that, he might not be dead yet, but it was only a matter of time and he wouldn't be doing any fighting in the interval before he crossed the divide.

The Kid climbed to his feet and leaned against the tree that had shielded him. Neither of the first two men he'd shot had moved since they fell, but that didn't mean for sure they were dead. As long as that uncertainty existed, he continued to regard them as potential threats.

The feeling was starting to return to his left arm and shoulder and he was able to hold the revolver in his left hand. Using his right to thumb fresh cartridges into the cylinder, The Kid quickly reloaded the empty Colt as he kept his eyes on the first two men on the ground. He was also very curious about the identity of whoever had called out and then shot the rifleman. That man had saved his life, but who he was or why he had taken a hand in the fight was unknown.

He snapped the Colt closed and walked over to the stocky man and the one in the derby.

The stocky man had fallen on his back with his arms flung out limply at his sides. He stared sightlessly at the sky with eyes glassy in death.

The derby-wearer was lying on his stomach. The Kid could see marks on the ground where the man's fingers had clawed against it in death spasms. Just to make sure, he kept the man covered, hooked a boot toe under his shoulder, and rolled him onto his back. His eyes were as glassy as those of his companion.

So it was a clean sweep, The Kid thought. Just one question remained, and it looked like it was about to be answered.

A man emerged from the trees farther along the creek and walked toward The Kid, leading a saddle horse with his left hand and carrying a Winchester in his right.

The Kid didn't holster his gun, despite the fact the stranger had helped him. It took more than that to earn his trust. He watched alertly, studying the man as he approached.

He moved along in a fairly spry fashion, but the man was getting on in years. Judging by the gray in his hair and the lines etched in his face, he had to be sixty, maybe even older. A mustache drooped over his mouth. He wore a gray Stetson and had a gray vest over his white shirt.

The Kid straightened a little as he saw the badge pinned to the stranger's vest.

The man gave him a friendly smile and asked, "Are you hurt, son?"

The Kid shook his head. "No, sir, I'm fine. A bullet glanced off the tin where I keep my matches and knocked me out of the saddle, but that's all."

"Well, that was mighty good luck, wasn't it?" The stranger chuckled as he came to a stop about ten feet away. "I've always said that a fast, steady hand and cool nerves are fine, but there's no substitute for pure, old-fashioned good luck."

The Kid returned the man's smile. "I can't argue with that, Marshal. Or is it Sheriff?"

"No, you were right the first time. It's Marshal. Marshal Jared Tate, from Copperhead Springs."

The name of the town was vaguely familiar to The Kid. He recalled seeing it on a map of Kansas pinned to the wall of an eatery in Dodge City. He'd examined it briefly while he was having his meal. Other than that, he'd never heard of the place.

As he remembered the map, Copperhead Springs was a good distance west of where he was. "I certainly appreciate the help, Marshal, but I'm curious. If you're a town marshal, what are you doing out here this far from your bailiwick?"

"Oh, I'm on my way back there, don't worry," Tate said. "I've been over to Fort Hays, delivering a prisoner to the army. Picked up a particularly vicious deserter called Brick Cantrell, and they were mighty glad to get him back." The lawman didn't lose his friendly smile or his mild tone, but a slight edge of steel crept into his voice as he went on. "No offense, son, but you know who I am and what I'm doing here, and I don't know a thing about you except that I killed a man to save your life."

"Sorry, Marshal. I should have introduced myself. My name's Morgan." The Kid paused. He had a reputation as a gunfighter, and a lot of badge-toters had begun to look at him suspiciously, as they had been doing with his father for decades. Still, he wanted to be honest with this man who had helped him. "Some people call me Kid Morgan."

If the name meant anything to Marshal Jared Tate, he gave no sign of it. He just nodded. "Pleasure to meet you, Mr. Morgan. Now that we've been properly introduced, you mind telling me why those hombres were trying to kill you?"

"They wanted to steal my horses. They'd already ridden one of their mounts to death, and the others weren't far from it."

"They must've been in a mighty big hurry. Any idea why?"

The Kid shook his head. "No, but if I had to guess, I'd say they were on the run from the law."

"I agree with you. When I heard all that

shooting, I figured I ought to take a look. Careful-like, you understand, because I didn't know what I'd be getting into. So I slipped along the creek for a ways. When I saw the odds were two against one, and those two telling my lawman's instincts that they were no good, I knew I needed to give you a hand. The way that fella with the rifle tried to bushwhack you just confirmed it."

"That was a good shot you made," The Kid said.

Tate shrugged, but The Kid could tell he was pleased to hear that.

"My eyes may be getting old, but they're still pretty sharp. Whereabouts are you headed, Mr. Morgan?"

The sudden question took The Kid a little by surprise, but he answered honestly. "No place in particular. I thought I might see if I could find a riding job on one of the ranches in this end of the state."

"Why don't you come along to Copperhead Springs with me?" Tate suggested. "I know just about everybody who has a spread around there. I'm sure it won't be hard to find one who needs a good hand."

That was another lucky break for The Kid. From what he could remember from that map, he estimated it was another couple days' ride to the settlement, and he wouldn't mind having some company. Tate obviously felt the same way.

"All right. I appreciate that, Marshal. I was

planning to make camp along this creek tonight, if you'd care to share my coffee and bacon and beans."

"That sounds like a good idea to me." Tate paused. "We might want to move a little farther upstream before we settle down for the night, though. I never cared much for sharing a camp-ground with dead folks."

Chapter 3

The Kid might have been tempted to leave the dead hardcases where they had fallen—there were enough coyotes and other scavengers around to take care of them—but Marshal Tate seemed to assume they were going to bury the men. The Kid didn't want to argue with the man who had saved his life, so he broke out his shovel and did the digging.

He put the four men in a single grave, and by the time he finished filling in the hole in the ground, night was falling.

"Don't worry, I can still find us a good camp-site, even in the dark," Tate said as they started west along the creek. "I've been all over this part of the country for years, know it like the back of my own hand."

The Kid was leading one of the extra horses, along with his pack animal. The marshal led the other two horses. As they rode at an easy pace along the stream, The Kid asked, "Have you been a lawman in other towns besides Copperhead Springs?"

"Oh, Lord, yes, a dozen or more. I was one of Hickok's deputies in Abilene, you know."

"Wild Bill himself?"

"That's right. I never really thought he was all that wild, except when circumstances forced him to be. Most of the time he seemed like a fine gentleman. It nearly broke my heart when I heard he'd been shot from behind by that coward up in Deadwood. If Bill had been facing the door, Jack McCall never would have got that close to him with a gun."

After a couple decades of estrangement, The Kid and his father had grown closer over the past few years. He had heard quite a few stories from Frank Morgan about the old days of the Wild West. He was interested to hear what else Jared Tate had to say. "Where else did you serve as a peace officer?"

"I was a Ford County deputy when Jim Masterson was the sheriff. Served alongside him and his brother Bat."

"Really? I know Bat Masterson."

"Is that so?" Tate laughed. "Well, it just goes to show you it's true what they say about how the West is really a small place despite all those wide open spaces. Bat's a fine man."

"He is," The Kid agreed, thinking of how Masterson had given him a hand during his cross-country quest. He wasn't going to let himself think too much about how that had turned out, but he wasn't going to forget the people who had helped him out along the way.

"Dodge City's where I met the Earps, too," Tate went on. "I wound up heading out to Arizona Territory some years back and spent some time in Tombstone while they were there. Fine bunch of boys, mind you, but . . . headstrong, I guess you could say. You didn't want to get on the wrong side of them."

"I've heard Wyatt Earp has gone up to Alaska to cash in on that gold rush."

"What gold rush?" Tate asked with a frown.

"They've found gold along some river up there called the Yukon. It caused a rush just like the one to California back in '49. You haven't heard about it?"

"Life's pretty slow in Copperhead Springs," Tate said with a smile. "And I've never been all that good about keeping up with the news. To me a newspaper's got its uses . . . but most of 'em involve the outhouse!"

The Kid laughed at that. As they rode on, Tate continued reminiscing about various places he had worn a star, most of them small towns in Kansas and Nebraska. "I like this part of the country, you know," he mused. "From time to time I might go someplace like Tombstone, just to see something new, but I always come back to these parts. It seems to me this is the heart of the country, and not just because it's in the middle. It's the beating heart, where the things that make this America are most honest and true."

The Kid supposed most people thought that was the case about where they lived, if they thought about such things at all, but he didn't say it to Marshal Tate. He just smiled and nodded.

A short time later they came to a spot along the creek perfect for camping, with an open space in the trees, level ground, plenty of grass for the horses, and an easy slope down to the stream. They picketed and unsaddled the horses, then The Kid gathered some wood to build a fire. There were enough broken cottonwood branches around to make it unnecessary to collect the dried buffalo chips usually needed to build a fire on the prairie.

"Let me boil the coffee," Tate suggested when flames were leaping merrily from the heap of branches The Kid had arranged. "You shouldn't have to use all your supplies."

"All right," The Kid agreed. "I'll fry up some bacon and heat the beans I've got leftover from last night."

Tate got a small coffeepot from the pack lashed behind his saddle. He carried it down to the stream to fill it with water.

The Kid noticed a couple minutes later that

Tate hadn't come back. He lifted his gaze from the thick strips of bacon beginning to sizzle in his frying pan and looked toward the creek. The glow from the fire reached that far, and The Kid could see Tate standing beside the stream, the coffeepot still in his hand hanging at his side.

"Marshal?" The Kid called. "Something wrong?"

Tate gave a little shake of his head, not like he was answering The Kid's question but more in the manner of a man waking up. He looked back over his shoulder. "What?"

"Is anything wrong?" The Kid repeated. "You were going to get water for the coffee."

"The coffee . . ." Tate lifted the pot and looked at it, then laughed. "Good Lord. The night's so plumb beautiful I reckon I just got caught up in it and forgot what I was doing. Thanks for the reminder, Mr. Morgan."

"You can call me Kid, Marshal. Most folks do."

Tate knelt to fill the pot. "Seems a mite disrespectful, calling a grown man Kid. Doesn't it bother you?"

"Not really. I've always figured Mr. Morgan is my father, not me."

He didn't add that his father was Frank Morgan, also known as The Drifter, the last of the famous Old West gunfighters. There were still plenty of men around who were fast on the draw and lived by the gun, but Frank was the only survivor of the old breed who still lived as he always had.

26

Some of the other famous shootists were still around, but they had all hung up their guns.

"Your father is still living, is he?" Tate asked as he came back to the fire with the coffeepot.

"Oh, yeah. At least as far as I know. We don't see each other all that often."

"There's not trouble between you, is there?" Tate asked with a small frown.

"No, not at all. At one time there was, but in the last few years . . . well, we've become good friends. We're just both too fiddle-footed to get together very often."

"I'm glad to hear it. You should enjoy all the time you do get to spend with him. It'll seem all too soon that he's gone."

The Kid shook his head. Frank Morgan was such a larger than life figure, it was impossible to imagine him not being around. Logically, of course, The Kid knew that was inevitable.

But he couldn't believe it in his heart.

He continued fixing the meal, and realized something several minutes later as he glanced at the coffeepot sitting at the edge of the fire. "Marshal, you didn't put the coffee in the pot, did you?"

"What? Why, sure, I—" Tate leaned forward and sniffed. "That doesn't smell like coffee. Come to think of it, I don't believe I did. I'm feeling a little absentminded tonight, Kid. Probably has something to do with shooting that man. To tell you the truth, it's been a while since I had to kill a man,

27

and it's never been something that sets easy on me."

"I understand." The Kid had seen so much violence he'd become a little hardened to it, but knew most people, even peace officers, weren't like that.

Tate got a sack of Arbuckle's from his gear and poured grounds into the pot. Soon the smell of the strong black brew filled the air, mingling well with the aroma of the bacon.

The food was good, and The Kid ate his fill, washing it down with the marshal's excellent coffee. When they were finished, since there was a creek handy he washed out the coffeepot, the skillet, and the pot he had used to heat the beans, which they had polished off. He put everything away, then sat down on the bedroll he had spread next to the fire.

Tate sat on the opposite side of the fire, packing tobacco in a pipe. When he had it ready, he fired it up, took a few puffs, and heaved a sigh of satisfaction. "I tell you, Kid, living in town is all right, but I like getting out here away from everybody sometimes. That's probably why I said I'd take Cantrell to Fort Hays and deliver him to the army. I knew it would give me a chance for a nice leisurely ride back to Copperhead Springs with a few nights on the trail."

"And then I came along and intruded on your privacy by nearly getting myself killed," The Kid said with a grin as he stretched out on the blankets and propped himself up on an elbow.

Tate waved the pipe in the air. "Oh, no, I'm not worried about that. A cheerful traveling companion is always welcome, as long as he's not the sort who jabbers all the time. I can already tell you're not that sort. You know how to be quiet and leave a man with his thoughts." Tate pointed the pipe's stem at him. "That's because you're a man with a lot of thoughts of your own."

That was certainly true, and The Kid was about to say as much when he heard something move in the darkness. It was just a faint sound, the scrape of leather against dirt, maybe, but his instincts picked it out from all the other sounds belonging around a trail camp.

Somebody was out there, and without having to think about it, The Kid moved his hand toward his gun.

"Hold it!" a man's voice commanded. "You better freeze, mister. You're covered, and if you pull that gun, I'll ventilate you."

Chapter 4

The Kid stopped before his fingers closed around the butt of the Colt. It wasn't easy to do so; his first impulse was to pull the gun and roll fast to the side, to throw off the aim of whoever was threatening him.

But Marshal Tate was sitting on the other side of the fire rather flat-footed, smoking his pipe, clearly not prepared for trouble. If bullets started flying, the old lawman might not survive.

The Kid was willing to give the situation a few seconds to see how it was going to play out. "Take it easy, mister," he called. "There's no need for gunplay here."

The unseen man responded with a snort. "I'll be the judge of that. Who are you?"

"I could ask the same of you," The Kid said.

"Yeah, but I'm the one holding a rifle aimed dead straight at your brisket. Now answer the question."

"My name's Morgan. And my friend is a lawman, in case you missed the star on his vest. His name's Tate."

Pointing out that Tate was a lawman was a calculated risk. If the unseen man threatening them was an outlaw, he might be prompted to start shooting.

On the other hand, if he was a law-abiding man he probably wouldn't feel very comfortable about pointing a rifle at a peace officer. That was what The Kid was hoping for, anyway.

That hope was rewarded as the man said, "Yeah, yeah, I see the badge now. All right to come in to the camp?"

"Just don't come in shooting," The Kid warned.

Crackles sounded in the brush along the creek

30

bank as a man stepped into the light holding a Spencer repeating rifle of the type carried by the U.S. cavalry. His faded blue trousers with remnants of yellow stripes down the legs appeared to be army issue, as was the gray hat with the turned-up brim he wore. His shirt was buckskin, though, and his high-topped boots were fashioned moccasin-style, rather than military. He was about the same age as Marshal Tate, with a weathered face and considerable gray in his brown hair and mustache.

He wore a badge, too, pinned to his buckskin shirt. He pointed the rifle at the ground. "Sorry about the misunderstanding. I thought you might be a couple of the hombres I've been trailing. I can see now that you're not. Maybe you've seen 'em, though."

The Kid was sitting up, alert. "Four men. A short, stocky bearded fella, a tall skinny one in an old derby hat, a redhead, and a man with a scar down his left cheek that looked like he got it in a knife fight."

The newcomer's eyes narrowed as he listened to those descriptions. He shifted the Spencer slightly, as if he were tempted to raise it and point it at him again. "You've seen them, all right, and up close, too. They happen to be friends of yours?"

"Not hardly," Tate said, speaking up for the first time. "We killed them a while ago."

"They're buried a few miles downstream." The Kid nodded in that direction.

The stranger looked surprised, although he tried to conceal that reaction. "I reckon you'd better tell me about it."

"I don't see why we should," Tate said crisply. "That's a town marshal's badge you're wearing, just like mine, and since I don't see any town around here, you're out of your jurisdiction."

"So are you," the man snapped, "but that didn't stop you from killing those hombres."

"They didn't give us much choice about it."

The Kid didn't particularly want to sit around and listen to the two old-timers squabble with each other. "Listen, why don't you two introduce yourselves, and then you can both share what you know about the situation."

The stranger shrugged. "That's all right with me, I suppose."

"Me, too." Tate stood up and extended his hand. "Marshal Jared Tate."

"Marshal Bob Porter," the other man said as he gripped Tate's hand. "I'm from a town called Chalk Butte, about thirty miles east of here."

The Kid had heard of Chalk Butte, but hadn't passed through there while he drifted west.

"I know Chalk Butte well, although it's been quite a while since I was there," Tate said. "I'm from Copperhead Springs."

"Copperhead Springs?" Porter repeated with a

frown. "But I thought . . . Nah, never mind. I want to hear about your run-in with those varmints. I have to say, I'm a mite surprised you're still alive. They are . . . or rather, they were, if you're telling me the truth . . . a vicious bunch."

"I don't doubt that for a second," The Kid said. "They tried to steal my horses because they had ridden one of theirs to death and the others were almost that far gone. I objected to having my horses stolen. Marshal Tate happened to come along and give me a hand with my objections."

"So you shot it out with those men, and they're dead and you're not?" Porter sounded like he had a hard time believing that.

"We brought along the three horses that were still alive," The Kid said, nodding toward where the animals were picketed. "If you know the mounts you've been chasing, maybe you'd recognize them."

"I might." Porter walked over to look at the horses. The Kid and Tate went with him.

After studying the horses in the firelight for a moment, Porter turned to them and nodded. "Sure looks like the animals they rode out of Chalk Butte on," he admitted. "I reckon you're probably telling the truth."

"We can show you the grave and you can dig them up if you want," The Kid said.

A grim smile curved Porter's mouth. "No, I don't think that'll be necessary. Did you, uh, happen to look in the saddlebags you took off those horses?"

"Haven't gotten around to it yet," Tate said. "They're piled over there on the ground. If there's stolen bank money or something like that, you'll find it there."

"What makes you think they had loot with them?"

"You chased them this far, and pretty hard and fast, too, judging by how worn out those horses were. You must have a pretty good reason for that."

"I do"—a grim look settled over Porter's face— "but it's not money. Those men abused and murdered a young woman. A friend of my daughter's in fact. I would've trailed them pretty much all the way to hell if I had to . . . if they hadn't run into you two first."

"Good Lord," Tate muttered. "That's awful. I didn't feel bad about killing them to start with because I knew they had to be owlhoots of some sort, but now I wish we'd made them suffer more."

"At least they're dead. It won't bring that poor girl back, but it's about as close to justice as we'll find in this world."

The three men stood in solemn silence for a moment, then The Kid said, "There might still be a little coffee in the pot, Marshal. You're welcome to join us if you want."

"I'm obliged for the invitation," Porter said with

a nod. "I'll take you up on it. When I saw your fire I left my horse about half a mile downstream. I'll fetch him and be back shortly."

"We don't have any supper left, but I can fry up some bacon while you're gone," The Kid offered.

"No need, but again, I'm obliged. I've still got plenty of jerky and biscuits I brought with me. I knew it might be a long chase."

Porter started down the creek while The Kid and Tate returned to the fire.

"What do you think?" The Kid asked. "Is he telling the truth about everything?"

"I believe so," Tate said. "I was pretty suspicious at first because I thought I knew all the lawmen in these parts and I'd never heard of him. The last I heard, a fella named Griggs was the marshal in Chalk Butte. But like I told Porter, that's been a few years. They could have changed marshals over there more than once in that time."

The Kid nodded. "He seems genuine enough to me, too."

"I'm going to keep an eye on him anyway," Tate said. "It never hurts to be careful."

Porter returned about a quarter hour later leading a saddled horse. He unsaddled the animal and picketed it with the others.

"We boiled some more coffee," Tate said, "so you won't have to drink the dregs."

"Mighty hospitable of you." Porter brought out his own cup, filled it from the pot, and settled down to make a late supper of jerky and biscuits he took from his supplies. Between bites, he said, "Reason I asked about those saddlebags is those men stole some jewelry from the girl they attacked. I'd like to be able to take it back to her family. It won't help much . . . hell, it won't help any, I expect . . . but at least losing it won't make matters even worse."

"It should still be there," The Kid assured him.

From the other side of the fire, Tate said, "I'm a little curious about something, Marshal."

"What's that?" Porter asked.

"Did you bring a posse with you?"

Porter shook his head. "No, this was a chore I wanted to handle myself. Like I said, the girl was a friend of the family."

"So those four hardcases were running away like the Devil himself was after them, when it was only one man?"

"I guess they didn't know I was by myself. Either that or they figured I was mad enough they didn't want me catching up to them, alone or not." Porter shook his head. "Let's face it, after what they'd done, they had to know there was no place they could hide. If they were ever caught, they'd be strung up. Even most other outlaws would've gunned them down like the hydrophobia skunks they were."

Tate nodded slowly. "That's true, I reckon."

Porter turned to The Kid. "I've been thinking. I

36

remember hearing a lot about a man named Morgan. A gunfighter. Just the sort of man who wouldn't think twice about throwing down on those badmen, even with four to one odds. But you seem mighty young to be him."

"You're talking about Frank Morgan," The Kid said.

"That's it. That's the name, all right."

"I'm not him." The Kid left it at that and didn't go into the details of his relationship to Frank Morgan.

"This is Kid Morgan," Tate added.

Porter smiled thinly. "Are you a gunfighter, too, Kid?"

"There are no wanted posters out on me, if that's what you're asking, Marshal."

"Can't blame an old lawman's instincts for kicking in." Porter took another drink of the coffee and nodded in satisfaction. "That's good. So we'll share this camp tonight and then go our separate ways in the morning? I'm anxious to get back home, and I expect you are, too, Marshal."

"That's right," Tate said.

"Copperhead Springs . . . Maybe I'll get over that way again one of these days."

"You'll be welcome," Tate assured him. "Copperhead Springs is a nice, friendly place."

Chapter 5

After a shared breakfast in the morning, the men saddled up and got ready to ride.

"Do you want those three horses that belonged to the men you were chasing?" Tate asked Marshal Bob Porter. "We don't really need them."

Porter shook his head. "No, I reckon they're rightfully yours now." He patted one of the saddlebags slung on his horse. "I got that jewelry I came after, and the only other thing I wanted was to see those scum brought to justice. You and The Kid here took care of that."

"Well, I'm glad we could help out, even though we didn't know at the time what they'd done."

Porter swung into the saddle and lifted a hand in farewell as he turned his horse. The Kid and Tate stood for a moment, watching him ride off to the east before they mounted up as well.

"It strikes me the marshal is a pretty good hombre," Tate commented. "And my years carrying a badge have given me a pretty good instinct for such things."

"I think you're right," The Kid said. "He seemed friendly enough, but if I was a lawbreaker I don't think I'd want him hunting me."

They pushed on west toward Copperhead

Springs. As they rode, The Kid asked Tate if he knew how the place got its name.

"As a matter of fact, I do. This was before I ever came to these parts, of course, but back when the wagon trains were coming through here, one group of immigrants decided to stop and settle at some springs they came to. A good supply of water is one of the most important things a town can have, and these springs looked like they'd been there for a long time and were in no danger of going dry. So the people figured they'd build a town around the springs.

"They hadn't been there long, though, before they realized the place was crawling, and I do mean *crawling,* with copperhead snakes. Several folks got bitten, and a couple even died.

"So the immigrants were faced with another decision. They could leave that perfect spot for a settlement, or they could stay and try to wipe out the snakes. They decided to stay and fight."

"I'm guessing they eventually got rid of the snakes?"

Tate nodded. "It took a long time, but the old-timers tell me nobody has seen a copperhead around there for more than twenty years. I know I've never seen one since I went there to be the marshal. Other kinds of snakes every now and then, but no copperheads. Which is fine with me, because I don't care for snakes, period."

"I don't, either," The Kid said. "I spent some

time once in a place called Rattlesnake Valley."

"Now that is somewhere I would not like to go," Tate drawled with a smile on his lined face.

"It's not quite as bad as it sounds, especially now that all the two-legged reptiles are cleaned out."

Tate glanced over at him. "You had something to do with that, I'm betting?"

"A little," The Kid admitted.

When they camped that night after an uneventful day, Tate said, "We ought to make the town by tomorrow evening. I'll be glad to get back."

"Do you have a deputy you left to take care of things while you were gone?" The Kid asked.

"Oh, sure. Deputy, uh . . . Deputy . . ." Tate laughed and shook his head. "If that don't beat all. I've had so many deputies they're getting all mixed up in my head. And this boy's almost like a son to me."

"Well, it doesn't really matter," The Kid said. "I'll be meeting him soon enough when we get there."

"Hope you'll stay around town for a while and take advantage of our hospitality. Copperhead Springs is one of the friendliest towns you'll ever find."

"I'm sure I'll be around if you can help me get a job on one of the ranches in the area," The Kid pointed out.

"You're looking for a riding job?"

"Yeah. I told you yesterday."

"Oh." Tate laughed again. "Well, I've slept since then, haven't I?"

"I guess we both have." The Kid broke out the skillet and the coffeepot and started preparing supper.

They slept well that night and were on the trail again early the next morning. Tate brought up the cowboying job The Kid hoped to get. "Since you mentioned it last night, I've been doing some thinking about it, and I think the place to start would be Cy Levesy's Broken Spoke Ranch. It's the biggest spread in the area, and Cy's a good friend of mine."

"I appreciate that," The Kid said.

"Of course, if Cy really doesn't need any hands right now, I'm sure he'd take you on anyway, as a favor to me, but I wouldn't ask him to do that."

The Kid shook his head. "I wouldn't want you to."

"There are plenty of other outfits around that might take you on. You won't be without work long, I guarantee that." Tate chuckled. "After seeing the way you can shoot, maybe I ought to hire you as my deputy. I could use a good man to take over when I'm gone."

"I thought you already had a deputy," The Kid said with a frown.

"What? Me? No, I've been keeping the peace alone in Cottonwood Springs for years now."

"Copperhead Springs."

"What about it?"

"You said Cottonwood Springs instead of Copperhead Springs."

Tate frowned and shook his head. "No, I don't think I did."

"I'm pretty sure—"

"Maybe you just heard me wrong. Copperhead, cottonwood, they're sort of similar sounding. That's all it was." Tate looked relieved and went on. "I should know what the town's called, since we were talking about Cy Levesy a few minutes ago and Cy's one of the old-timers in those parts. He told me the story about how a wagon train full of immigrants on their way west came to the springs and decided to stop there. A town needs a good supply of water, you see, and those springs were good and strong and looked like they'd been there a long time. They weren't likely to dry up any time soon. But it wasn't long after those folks decided to settle there that they discovered the place was crawling, and I mean *crawling,* with copperheads. Mean, nasty snakes those are, let me tell you. They bit some of the settlers, and a few of those poor people died. So they were faced with the choice of moving on and leaving those springs behind, or staying and trying to get rid of the snakes, because other than that, the place was perfect for a town. What do you think they did?"

Slowly, trying not to frown, The Kid said,

"They decided to stay and wipe out the snakes?"

Tate grinned and slapped his thigh as he rode along easy in the saddle. "That's exactly what they did! It took a while, mind you, years, in fact, before they got rid of all those scaly little devils, but folks who have been around there for a long time, like Cy Levesy, tell me it's been twenty years or more since anybody saw a copperhead around."

"Maybe they should change the name of the town to No Copperhead Springs," The Kid said.

That brought a pleased laugh from Tate. "That's a good one. It surely is. I'll have to tell Cy what you said, Mister . . . uh . . ."

"Just call me Kid."

"Sure, Kid. Anyway, I'll tell Cy. That's a good one."

The Kid turned his head and stared off into the distance. He didn't want Tate to see the bleak look he knew was in his eyes.

In the roughly day and a half he had known the marshal he had noticed several times that Tate seemed to be a mite absentminded. At first The Kid hadn't thought anything about it. Everybody could be forgetful at times. Even someone as young and healthy as he was had things slip his mind.

But Tate seemed more muddled than he had been the day before, from not being able to remember his deputy's name—if he even had a deputy—to forgetting the name of the town where he lived, to telling The Kid the same story about the origin of the town's name as if he had no memory of spinning the same yarn the night before. It was troubling to think a man could forget so much.

If he couldn't remember such basic things, how could anyone know if anything he'd said had been true?

The Kid glanced over at his companion, specifically at the badge pinned to Tate's vest.

How could he be sure Tate was really a lawman? The badge looked real . . . the badge might *be* real . . . but did Tate really have the right to wear it?

And if he did, what sort of town would hire a man with obvious mental problems to keep the peace?

The Kid didn't know, but he suspected he would find out. He knew Copperhead Springs existed because he had seen it on that map, which was a recent one, as he recalled. For the same reason, he knew they were headed in the right direction to reach the settlement. The best thing to do, he decided, was to keep riding along with Tate and see what happened when they got there.

One thing he knew was he couldn't ride off and leave the man alone out on the prairie. The shape he was in, there was no telling what might happen to him.

Although Tate had been plenty capable when it came to gunplay, The Kid reminded himself. He had drilled that outlaw and saved The Kid's life.

Obviously there were some things Tate hadn't forgotten.

Late that afternoon, they topped a ridge and The Kid was able to look down into a green valley watered by a narrow, meandering stream flowing from a large pool on the far side of the valley. Sunlight reflected brilliantly from the surface of the pool, which was no doubt fed by those springs. Between stomping snakes, those early settlers must have figured out a way to trap some of the flow from the springs to form the pool.

The settlement itself lay just to the south of the springs. To the north was a beautiful parklike area. The town was good sized consisting of four main streets running parallel to each other for half a dozen blocks, with the corresponding cross streets. The Kid saw a couple church steeples, a large brick building at the edge of town that was probably the school, and some substantial-looking businesses in the downtown area.

A nice place to live, Tate had claimed, and The Kid could believe that, at least, judging by what he saw as the two of them approached. Peaceful, Tate had called it.

But maybe not.

A flurry of gunshots suddenly erupted, and as

the ominous crackle drifted through the late afternoon air, Tate stiffened and leaned forward in the saddle. "Trouble!" he exclaimed. "And in my town! I'll put a stop to that!"

Tate dropped the reins of the extra horses he'd been leading and kicked his own mount into a run, ignoring The Kid's urgent "Marshal! Wait!"

Too late. Whatever the trouble was, Tate was charging right into the middle of it.

And The Kid had no real choice but to go straight after him.

Chapter 6

The Kid dropped the reins of the pack horse and the extra saddle mount, then sent the buckskin galloping after Tate. The trail turned into the main street of Copperhead Springs. The shots were coming from the center of town.

Tate reined in about fifty feet in front of The Kid and swung down smoothly from the saddle, his feet hitting the ground before his horse ever stopped moving. The marshal might have trouble remembering some things, but he was still mighty spry for his age.

He had come to a halt in front of the Trailblazer Saloon, which appeared to be a large, successful establishment. By the time The Kid reined in and dismounted, Tate had bounded up the steps to the boardwalk. Gun in hand, he started toward the saloon's batwing entrance.

The shots had stopped for the time being, but they might start again without any warning, especially if Tate charged in there blindly with his gun drawn. As the lawman reached the bat wings, The Kid called after him, "Marshal, maybe you'd better—"

With a crash of glass, a man came flying through one of the saloon's front windows. He landed on the boardwalk, rolled under the railing, and dropped off the edge, landing limply on the ground with a heavy thud.

Tate had paused with his left hand on one side of the bat wings, ready to thrust it open. He turned his head to stare in surprise at the man crashing through the window. Before the marshal could start inside again, a big man bulled his way through the doorway, slapping the bat wings aside.

The swinging doors smacked into Tate and drove him back a step. One of his boot heels caught on the planks of the boardwalk, and he lost his balance and sat down hard.

The man sneered at Tate. "Better watch where you're going, Grandpa."

Anger welled up inside The Kid. "No, you're the one who'd better watch out, mister."

The man glared murderously as he swung his head around to look at The Kid. He was huge, with slab-muscled shoulders seemingly as broad

47

as an ox-yoke, long, gorilla-like arms, and a big gut that looked soft but probably wasn't. Black stubble covered his cheeks, and his hat was pushed back on a thatch of equally coarse black hair.

"What'd you say, mister?" he demanded in a rumbling voice.

"I said you should watch where you're going," The Kid snapped. "That man you just knocked down is the marshal of Copperhead Springs."

A bark of laughter came from the big man. "What, that old fool?"

Tate made a lunging grab for the revolver he had dropped when he fell. "I'll show you who's an old fool, you big lummox!"

The big man's face went from being arrogant and mildly amused to cold, vicious, and ruthless in an instant. He drew back a leg that seemed as big as a tree trunk, and The Kid knew he was about to kick Tate before the old lawman could reach the fallen gun.

In a blur of speed, The Kid palmed out his Colt and pointed it at the big man. Even though the Colt was a double-action, his thumb looped over the hammer and drew it back.

Something about the sound of a gun being cocked froze the blood of most men.

"Don't do it," The Kid warned. "I'll put a bullet in you before I let you hurt that man."

The big man trembled a little from the need to lash out that obviously gripped him. He said between clenched teeth, "You don't know what you're doin'."

"I'm helping a friend," The Kid said. His voice was hard and flat. "Marshal, can you get up?"

"Of course I can get up," Tate snapped. He snatched his gun from the boardwalk and scrambled to his feet. "I'm not hurt. I just tripped and lost my balance."

"That's good," The Kid said. "Maybe you'd better go check on that fella who got thrown through the window." Ever since he'd gotten his first glimpse of the massive hombre he was covering at the moment, he'd had a pretty good idea what had happened. He didn't know who had fired the shots, though.

Tate went down the steps and hurried over to the man who still lay huddled in the street next to the boardwalk. He knelt beside the still figure and rolled it over.

A moment later, Tate lifted his head and announced in grim tones, "This man's dead, Kid. He's been shot three times."

"Self-defense," the big man rumbled. He hadn't moved since The Kid threw down on him, but his eyes burned brightly with hatred. "You can ask anybody in the saloon. They'll tell you."

The Kid had a hunch the people in the saloon would say whatever they thought this monster wanted them to say. A number of pale, worried faces were looking through the windows, intently

49

watching the tense confrontation on the board-walk, but taking no part in it.

Likewise, the street had cleared quickly as the trouble developed. The Kid sensed he and Tate were on their own.

For the moment, the situation was under control. The townspeople might be too scared to help him and Tate, but as long as they weren't interfering, The Kid figured he and the old lawman could take care of themselves.

Tate came back over to the steps. "I'll ask the people in the saloon, all right. I'll ask anybody who'll talk to me. And I'll get to the bottom of this, I can promise you that much, mister. But I'll do it after I've locked you up."

The big man frowned at him. "What are you talkin' about? You can't lock me up!"

"We'll see about that. What's your name?"

"You don't know who I am?" The big man sounded like he couldn't believe that.

"If I knew, I wouldn't be asking, now would I?" Tate snapped. "Tell me your name, blast it."

"I'm Jed Ahern," the man said. "Ramrod out at the Broken Spoke, you old fool."

"Keep a civil tongue in your head. You're already looking at a possible murder charge."

"It was self-defense, I tell you!"

Tate went on as if he hadn't heard the inter-ruption. "And it won't do you any good to lie about where you work. Ed McAfee's the foreman

50

at the Broken Spoke. I've known him for years."

"Ed . . . who?"

A bad feeling was starting to stir inside The Kid again. "Marshal, we can hash this out later. Maybe we'd better get this fella locked up."

Tate nodded. "That's a good idea."

"Which way's the jail?"

"Why, it's right down . . ." Tate's voice trailed off as he began to look around in confusion.

The Kid had suspected as much.

The marshal's office and jail was probably somewhere along Main Street. The town wasn't so big they couldn't find it.

He had a feeling it wasn't Tate's office anymore, though—which left the question of where the actual marshal of Copperhead Springs might be.

"Come on," The Kid ordered Ahern.

The big man shook his head and stayed where he was, his legs planted firmly on the boardwalk like the tree trunks they resembled.

"You're loco. I'm not goin' anywhere with you. You don't have any right to arrest me. You're the ones breakin' the law, not me."

"You see that badge on the marshal's vest?"

"I see a hunk of tin," Ahern said, sneering again. "It don't mean nothin' to me. He ain't the marshal here, so he's got no right to arrest me."

"Now I know you need to be locked up, saying I'm not the marshal," Tate shot back. "You're not in your right mind." He gestured with the gun in his hand. "Now, are you coming along peacefully, or do I have to buffalo you and drag you?"

It would take a horse and a rope to drag the massive Ahern, The Kid thought. Also, if the big man's skull was as solid and sturdy as the rest of him appeared to be, they might have to wallophim with a pistol barrel half a dozen times to knock him out, and he doubted Ahern would cooperate in the process that long. It was getting to the point where they might have to shoot him in the leg, and that had the potential to be pretty messy.

A swift drumming of hoofbeats suddenly sounded along the street. Somebody was in a mighty big hurry. Tate turned his head to look.

With shocking speed in such a massive, ape-like figure, Ahern made a move, leaping toward Tate. One of his big paws batted aside the marshal's gun before Tate could pull the trigger.

The Kid couldn't risk a shot. Ahern and the old lawman were too close together.

Ahern's hands clamped down on Tate's shoulders. Whirling, he literally threw Tate at The Kid, much like he must have thrown the dead man through the saloon window. The Kid tried to leap aside but couldn't avoid the impact as Tate crashed into him. The collision knocked The Kid off his feet, and he crashed onto the boardwalk on his back.

With a roar, Ahern leaped at him, clearly intending to stomp him to death.

Chapter 7

With doom literally looming above him, The Kid moved fast, throwing himself to the side and flinging his hands up to grab the boot Ahern was trying to plant in the middle of his face. With a loud grunt of effort, he heaved on it.

If Ahern hadn't had one foot in the air, The Kid probably wouldn't have been able to budge his massive weight. As it was, Ahern let out a startled yell as he suddenly found himself tipping toward the edge of the boardwalk. He fell against the railing and crashed right through it with a splintering of wood.

The Kid rolled onto hands and knees and quickly pushed himself to his feet. He knew falling off the boardwalk wouldn't be enough to put Ahern out of the fight.

The Kid took a quick glance at Tate. The marshal had struggled to a sitting position on the boardwalk next to the saloon's front wall. His hat had flown off and he'd dropped his gun again, but he seemed to be all right.

The Kid's attention shifted back to Ahern.

The big man was fighting his way up through the cloud of dust puffing around him in the street. He bellowed, "You! I'm gonna kill you!"

With nimble speed that was so surprising, he

leaped onto the boardwalk and charged The Kid, throwing a looping right.

The Kid was fast, too, and ducked under the blow. He stepped in close to hook a left and a right into the big target that was Ahern's belly. As he suspected, the man's gut was prominent, but it wasn't that soft. Ahern didn't seem to even feel the punches.

Using the same arm he had missed with, Ahern brought it sweeping back around. The Kid twisted and raised his shoulder so Ahern's forearm crashed into it instead of the side of his head. If the strike had found its intended target, it might have broken The Kid's neck.

As it was, the impact knocked him off his feet and sent him flying against the wall of the saloon.

The Kid bounced off and staggered, and before he could catch his balance, Ahern was on him again. Seeing the giant's arms opened wide, he dragged in a deep breath as he was caught in a bear hug.

It was just about the worst thing that could happen. The Kid's speed and quickness were the only advantages he had, and those didn't amount to much against Ahern. He was so much quicker than The Kid had expected.

As long as he was trapped inside the circle of Ahern's arms, The Kid had no real weapons and only a few moments before he ran out of air.

Those moments might just postpone the

inevitable. Ahern was strong enough to break his ribs and crush the life out of him.

The monster's grip never loosened as he picked up The Kid, gusting foul, whiskey-laden breath into The Kid's face from a distance of mere inches. "Not so damn smart now, are you?" Ahern jeered as he glowered at him.

The Kid's ribs seemed to groan and creak under Ahern's tremendous pressure. His head spun. He knew he might pass out, and if he did, more than the fight would be over.

His life probably would be, too.

He had one weapon left, he realized suddenly. Jerking his head back, he quickly drove it forward, lowering it so the crown of his forehead slammed into Ahern's nose.

The man screamed like a little girl.

That unexpected reaction prompted The Kid to strike again the same way. He felt the hot gush of blood over his forehead as the cartilage inside the big man's nose collapsed with an ugly crunching sound.

Howling in pain, Ahern pressed both hands to his nose as blood bubbled from it, and The Kid dropped four or five inches to the boardwalk. He stumbled as he landed and almost fell, but slapped a hand against the wall and kept himself upright.

A second later, that racket broke off as the big man came barreling at The Kid like a runaway train. His blood-smeared face was like something out of a nightmare . . . or something that would *give* somebody nightmares.

The Kid waited until the last possible second to move, then threw himself aside. Ahern plowed into the saloon wall at full speed. The Trailblazer Saloon was well built. The wall shivered slightly, but the building didn't fall down. Ahern bounced off and stumbled backward toward the edge of the boardwalk again.

The Kid helped him along by bending sideways at the waist, lifting his right foot, and driving the heel of his boot into Ahern's stomach.

The railing, already broken, wasn't there to slow him as he flew off the boardwalk. His arms flailed wildly, but there was nothing for him to catch. He landed a good ten feet from the edge of the boardwalk, with a sound much like a boulder would have made had it been dropped from a height. He didn't moan, didn't writhe, didn't try to get up. His hands and feet twitched a couple of times, and then he lay still.

The Kid looked around to see if Tate was still all right. He saw the old lawman standing a few yards away, but Tate was no longer alone. A tall, rawboned man stood with him and he had a gun in his hand.

The Kid's Colt was gone. He had dropped it sometime during the ruckus, and while he was sure it was nearby he couldn't see it.

Anyway, he wouldn't have wanted to draw on

the man with Tate, but that fella was wearing a badge, too.

Tate said, "Are you all right, uh . . . uh . . . ?" He had forgotten The Kid's name again.

Hesitating a moment to catch his breath, The Kid said, "Yeah, I reckon I'm fine, Marshal. My ribs'll be a little sore from that bear hug, but Ahern didn't break any of them."

"You're lucky, mister," the younger badge-toter said. "Jed Ahern has squeezed the life plumb out of more than one man."

That news didn't surprise The Kid, having felt the strength of Ahern's grip.

"Why isn't he in prison, then?"

The man shrugged. "They were fair fights. As fair as any fight between Ahern and a human being could be, I guess. Although to really be fair, he'd have to be fighting a grizzly bear or a mountain lion."

The Kid pointed to the body still lying in the street near the boardwalk. "I'm pretty sure he shot that man, then threw him out the window for good measure."

"Did you actually see that happen?"

"Well, no," The Kid admitted, "but there were a lot of shots in the saloon, and then just as the marshal and I got here, the body came flying out through the window. Ahern sauntered out just a second or two later, obviously pleased with himself."

"But you didn't actually *see* him hurt anybody, is that right?"

"No," The Kid snapped. "Not until he attacked the marshal and me when we tried to take him to jail." He wondered why Tate was staring at the boardwalk with a confused frown on his face instead of speaking up.

"That's another thing," the younger lawman said. "You keep calling old Jared here the marshal, when he's not. He hasn't been for several years now."

The Kid had been afraid of that. His worry was confirmed.

"Not true," Tate muttered without looking up. "I'm the marshal of Copperhead Springs. I'm the marshal."

"No, Jared, I am, remember? Riley Cumberland?"

Tate still didn't look up, but he shook his head stubbornly. "I'm the marshal."

Cumberland looked at The Kid. "Look, mister, I reckon I can give you the benefit of the doubt if you thought you were lending a helping hand to a real lawman, but you weren't. Jared retired as the town's marshal four years ago when he started getting forgetful. If you've been around him for very long at all, you'll have seen how easily he gets confused."

"I've seen it," The Kid said, his face and voice grim. "I also saw him save my life a few days ago."

"Well, I don't doubt it a bit. Jared was a mighty

fine lawman in his time, and on his good days, I guess he can still handle himself pretty well." Cumberland's voice hardened. "But he's got no right to arrest anybody anymore. I don't even know what he's doing here. He's supposed to be in Wichita, living with his daughter Bertha."

Tate brightened a little at the mention of that name. "Bertha. That's my little girl, Kid." His memory of who The Kid was had come back to him. "I'll introduce you to her. Cute as a button, she is. Just turned seven."

There was nothing The Kid could do but nod. "That's fine, Marshal. I'm looking forward to it."

Cumberland sighed. "You see what I mean. Now, I reckon I'd better get this mess cleaned up. It's a fine thing for a man to get back to town and find something like this waiting for him."

The Kid had already figured out Cumberland was the one who'd come galloping up just before the fight with Jed Ahern broke out. "Are you going to lock up Ahern until you find out what happened?"

"I can't lock up a man just on your say-so, mister," Cumberland replied. "And since you already told me you didn't see him do anything wrong—"

"I did," a new voice said. A woman's voice. She pushed the bat wings aside and stepped out of the saloon. "I saw Ahern shoot and kill Ed Phillips, and I'm willing to testify to it in a court of law."

Chapter 8

Marshal Riley Cumberland looked pained. "Damn it, Constance, you know that's not a very smart thing to do."

"What's not smart?" the woman demanded. "Telling the truth? Or expecting you to do your job, even if it means stirring up Harlan Levesy?"

"You got no call to talk that way," Cumberland snapped.

Tate looked up at the tall young lawman beside him and asked, "Why would you be worried about upsetting Harlan Levesy? He's a little boy."

Cumberland ignored him. "I always do my job, but there's nothing wrong with making sure what happened and not jumping to any conclusions."

"Oh, no," Constance said, her voice edged with bitter sarcasm. "You wouldn't want to jump to the conclusion that the Broken Spoke crew is nothing but a bunch of no-good hardcases now."

She was a big, middle-aged woman, seemingly almost as broad as she was tall, with red hair and a pugnacious expression on her round face. She wore a high-necked, long-sleeved gown of dark green silk and, due to the powerful nature of her personality, cut an impressive figure.

She wasn't the sort of woman he would want to

cross, The Kid decided. She looked like she could break most hombres in two.

The Kid picked up his hat, knocked some of the dust off of it, and settled it on his head. "You go right ahead and find out what happened, Marshal. Sounds like you've got an eyewitness right here."

Cumberland glared at him for a second, then holstered his revolver and said to Constance, "All right, go ahead and tell me about it."

"Ed Phillips was in my place having a drink when Ahern came in. He was proddy as ever—"

"Phillips, you mean?" Cumberland interrupted.

She gave him a scathing look. "Did you ever know Ed Phillips to be proddy in your life?" she demanded. "The man wouldn't hardly step on a scorpion! No, I'm talking about Ahern. He was looking to pick a fight, the same way he is about half the time when he comes into town, and his eyes happened to light on Ed this time."

While Constance was talking, Tate edged away from Cumberland and came over to The Kid. "None of this makes any sense, Kid," he said quietly. "There's some sort of trickery going on. Cy Levesy would never hire a man like Ahern, and his boy Harlan couldn't. Shoot, Harlan's only ten or twelve years old!"

Tate was lost in the past again, The Kid thought. He wasn't sure the old lawman was ever fully in the present anymore. "We'll see what they have to say, Marshal."

"Be careful. Folks will try to put one over on you."

"Well, I've got you to steer me right," The Kid said.

Tate smiled and nodded. "You sure do."

Constance was saying, "Ed knew what sort of varmint Ahern is, so he tried to put up with the man picking at him. Ed tried to leave, but Ahern wouldn't let him. Finally Ed just couldn't stand it anymore. He threw a punch at Ahern . . . That's when Ahern shot him."

"Phillips didn't reach for his gun?" Cumberland asked with a frown.

"No, he didn't. He swung his fist, that's all. I reckon if Ahern had beaten him to death then, he could've claimed self-defense, although that would've been a stretch since he's twice Ed's size. But that's not what happened. For some reason Ahern pulled first.

"Ed made a fight of it, though. He didn't go down right away, and managed to get his gun out after he was hit and got some shots off. Everybody in the place went diving for cover. It was a pretty good battle for a minute or so, but that's all. Ahern wasn't even hit, but poor Ed was shot to pieces. Then Ahern picked up Ed's body, made some comment about how it wasn't worth scraping his knuckles on trash like that, and chunked him through my window. That's the story, Marshal . . . and I say it's murder."

The Kid thought so, too. From the sound of it, even if Phillips had drawn first, his death would have still been murder. Maybe not legally, but certainly morally.

With the eyewitness testimony he had just heard, there was no question Ahern was legally guilty of murder and ought to hang for it. The members of a jury hadn't decided that yet . . . but they would if they got the chance.

They would if Marshal Cumberland locked up Ahern and held him for trial. That was what it amounted to.

Cumberland didn't seem to be disposed to do that, however. He was obviously looking for a way out of the dilemma when he asked, "Did anybody else in the saloon see things the same way, Constance?"

"Did anybody . . . They *all* saw it that way, if they were looking, because that's what happened!"

"You won't mind if I ask them to back up your story, then? Otherwise it's just your word."

"Which ought to be good enough." Constance scowled and turned to look over the bat wings. "Somebody come out here and tell this pitiful excuse for a marshal that Ahern murdered Ed Phillips!"

No one came out of the saloon.

Constance grabbed the bat wings and jerked them open.

"I said come out here and tell the truth!" she bellowed.

The Kid looked past her into the barroom. He could see a lot of pale, nervous faces, faces that were lowered or turned away so their owners wouldn't have to look directly at Constance.

"If you want to keep drinking here, you'll tell the marshal what happened!"

Not even that threat was enough to make any of the saloon's patrons budge.

But one man did come to the door. He was short and slender, wearing an apron over a stained white shirt and dark pants and carrying a mop. His thinning hair was almost colorless.

"It was like Miss Constance said, Riley," he told the marshal in a mild, hesitant voice. "Jed Ahern picked the fight, and he didn't wait for Mr. Phillips to draw. It was murder, all right."

"Well, of course you're gonna agree with her," Cumberland said. "You're the swamper here at the Trailblazer. You work for her."

"But it's the truth," the man insisted. "Doesn't your own father's word mean anything to you, Riley?"

The Kid's eyebrows lifted in surprise. He could tell from the flush creeping across Cumberland's face the swamper was telling the truth about being the marshal's father. Nobody else seemed surprised, so The Kid figured the relationship was common knowledge around Copperhead Springs.

One of the saloon's customers, a man with a thick white mustache, muttered, "Well, hell," then stepped forward to join Constance and the swamper on the boardwalk. "I'm tired of letting the Broken Spoke run roughshod over everybody in town. It's all true, what they said, Marshal. Ahern murdered Ed Phillips, and you really ought to lock him up."

Cumberland was starting to look sick. The Kid knew what he was thinking. Tate had told him the Broken Spoke was the biggest ranch in the area, which meant the man who owned it was probably the most powerful man in those parts. Apparently that was Harlan Levesy, the son of Cy Levesy, Marshal Tate's old friend. If The Kid had to guess, he'd say it was likely Cy was dead and Harlan had inherited the Broken Spoke.

Inherited it, hired a hardcase crew ramrodded by the brutal Jed Ahern, and set out to tighten his grip even more. The Kid had seen similar setups in the past and had heard about more of them from Frank Morgan, who had stepped in to help out folks against range hogs on numerous occasions.

However, none of that was really any of The Kid's business. He had come to Copperhead Springs because Jared Tate had saved his life during the run-in with those outlaws. It was up to the people of the town to settle their own problems.

Although . . . after that battle with Ahern, The Kid sort of had a personal grudge against the big man. It sure wouldn't break his heart to see Ahern behind bars, or dangling from a hang rope, for that matter. That was what he deserved.

At the moment, Ahern was starting to stir, moving his arms and legs where he lay in the street and turning his head from side to side.

"You'd better make up your mind what you're going to do, Marshal," The Kid said. "Ahern's waking up. If you're going to put him in jail, you'll probably have an easier time of it while he's still groggy."

"This stranger's right," Constance said. "You've got three witnesses accusing Ahern of murder. Isn't that enough to justify locking him up?"

"Four witnesses," another townsman said as he stepped out of the saloon. "It's time we got some sand in our craw again. Past time, maybe."

Several other men crowded just inside the saloon's entrance started to mutter, and Cumberland realized where things were going. "All right, all right. We'll lock him up, and the law can run its course. Somebody give me a hand with him."

Nobody appeared to be eager to do that, but The Kid didn't mind. "What do you want me to do?"

"Let me get some rope from my horse," Cumberland said. "Roll him onto his belly. I want him tied up good and tight before we try to move him down to the jail."

The Kid approached Ahern carefully. The man's eyes were still closed, but the eyelids were starting to flutter a little. He would regain consciousness soon.

With a grunt of effort, The Kid rolled Ahern onto his belly. Cumberland hurried over with a length of rope. He pulled Ahern's arms behind his back and lashed the thick wrists together, pulling the rope pretty tight.

"Let's sit him up." Cumberland and The Kid raised Ahern to a sitting position, and Cumberland wrapped the rest of the rope around and around the man's massive torso, finally tying it off so Ahern couldn't move his arms.

Ahern's head hung forward. He shook it back and forth, and a rumble like the sound of distant drums grew inside him. It came out in a grated curse as he lifted his head and stared around him in obvious confusion. "What the hell!" he roared. He struggled to move, but couldn't budge his arms.

"Take it easy, Ahern," Cumberland told him. "You're under arrest."

"Arrest! What the hell for?"

"Murder," Cumberland said. "You killed Ed Phillips."

"That . . . that little gnat? Killin' him ain't murder. That's more like . . . like steppin' on a piddlin' little bug!"

Constance said, "You see, Marshal, he admits it."

"That's not exactly what it sounded like to me," Cumberland snapped. He took hold of the rope and nodded for The Kid to do likewise. "We need to get him on his feet. Heave him up in one . . . two . . . three!"

It was a little like lifting a mountain, The Kid thought, but they managed.

"Help me get him down to the jail."

"What about Marshal Tate?"

From the boardwalk, the swamper said, "We'll take care of him, mister. Most of us here remember Jared. We'll look after him just fine. He'll be here later."

The Kid nodded. "I'm obliged." To Cumberland, he added, "Your father's a good man."

"He's a damned saloon swamper," the marshal snapped. "Don't talk to me about him."

"Whatever you say." That was none of his business, either, The Kid thought.

Holding on to the rope keeping Ahern bound, they forced him toward the jail. Ahern lunged back and forth in an attempt to pull free.

Cumberland drew his gun. "Damn it, I'll knock you out again if I have to, Ahern!" he warned. "Then we'll hitch a mule to you and drag you like the side of beef you are."

"You're gonna be sorry you did this, Marshal." Ahern glared back and forth between Cumberland and The Kid. "When the Broken Spoke gets through with you, you're gonna be sorry you was ever born!"

"Too late," Cumberland said. "Most of the time I already am."

Chapter 9

It took some doing, but The Kid and Marshal Cumberland managed to wrestle Ahern down Main Street, around the corner, into the jail, and finally into a cell. By the time the iron-barred door clanged shut with Ahern on the other side of it, The Kid felt like he'd been digging ditches all day.

"You can't just leave me all trussed up like this!" Ahern bellowed at them through the bars. He was fully conscious again and practically foaming at the mouth with rage.

"Turn around and back up against the bars," Cumberland told him. "It'll mean ruining a perfectly good piece of rope, but I'll cut you loose."

Ahern stood there glaring for a couple seconds, then did what Cumberland told him. The marshal took a clasp knife from his pocket, opened it, and reached through the bars with the blade to saw the ropes loose. As the pieces of lasso fell away, The Kid knelt, reached through the bars, and retrieved them.

"Can't even feel my damn hands," Ahern complained when his arms were free. "You didn't have any call to tie me that tight."

"I've seen what you can do when you get mad, Ahern," Cumberland said. "I wasn't taking any chances."

"You never seen me when I was really mad. Not like now. But that ain't the worst of it. Harlan ain't gonna stand for one of his boys bein' treated like this."

"Let me worry about Harlan Levesy."

Ahern threw back his head and laughed. "Oh, you better worry! You better worry a lot!"

With his mouth twisting like he'd bitten into something sour, Cumberland jerked his head toward the cell block door and motioned for The Kid to go ahead of him into the office at the front of the building.

The marshal heaved a sigh as he sank into a swivel chair behind a paper-cluttered desk. "Did I ever get your name, mister?"

"It's Morgan," The Kid said.

"How in the world did you wind up in Copperhead Springs with old Jared Tate?"

"I ran into the marshal a couple days east of here."

"He's not a marshal anymore." Cumberland's voice had a tone of irritated impatience to it.

"That's the way he introduced himself to me, so that's the way I think of him."

Cumberland took off his hat and expertly tossed it onto a hook attached to the wall behind him. "He's not in his right mind, you know. Can't remember anything anymore."

"He knows who he is . . . or who he was, anyway," The Kid pointed out.

Cumberland shrugged. "Yeah, but from what I hear, some days he doesn't even know his own daughter, and he lives with her . . . and she takes care of him. I'll bet she wasn't watching him close enough, and he wandered off and didn't know how to get back to her place."

"That's in Wichita, you said?"

"Yeah."

"So he was able to make it all the way across the state, almost back to his old hometown, traveling by himself," The Kid pointed out. "That doesn't sound to me like a man who's not in his right mind."

Cumberland grimaced. "Tate can take care of himself most of the time. He just thinks it's twenty years ago. So I'm not surprised he made it that far. If it's something he knew how to do back then, he still knows how to do it . . . mostly. His daughter and my sister were friends when the Tates still lived here. Edna gets letters from Bertha now and then. Bertha says her pa's forgetting more and more things these days, simple things that he used to do all the time."

Like how to put coffee in a coffeepot, The Kid

71

thought, suddenly remembering the first night he and Tate had spent on the trail.

"I don't guess any of that really matters," Cumberland went on. "He's here, and there are people like my pa who will look after him until we can figure out what to do with him. Jared Tate is just about the least of my worries right now."

"With Ahern being the biggest worry?"

"With Ahern's *boss* being the biggest worry."

The Kid didn't much like Marshal Riley Cumberland, but the bleak look in the marshal's eyes almost made him feel sorry for the man. He reminded himself that Cumberland would have been willing to look the other way when it came to Ed Phillips's murder. He wanted to know why.

"Harlan Levesy's got this town treed, doesn't he?"

"Not Levesy himself, but the men who work for him." Cumberland paused. "I guess it's pretty much the same thing, isn't it?"

"Pretty much," The Kid agreed.

Cumberland swung the chair from side to side a little as he said, "Tell me again, what business is this of yours?"

"None, I suppose. I'm just a drifter, thought I might look for a riding job in these parts. After I met up with Marshal Tate, he said he'd put in a good word for me with Cy Levesy, the owner of the Broken Spoke."

"Cy died two years ago."

"I'm not surprised to hear it."

"His boy took over the ranch," Cumberland continued. "Harlan never got along that well with the old man. They had different ideas about how things should be run. Cy started the Broken Spoke and built it into a successful spread, but Harlan thought it could be bigger, make even more money."

"So he started making things hard for some of the smaller outfits around him, and when the owners pulled out, he took over."

Cumberland's eyes narrowed with suspicion as he looked at The Kid. "You talk like a man who's been around some."

The Kid shrugged.

"You sure you didn't come here to hire your gun to Harlan Levesy, instead of looking for a riding job?" Cumberland asked.

"I never even heard of Harlan Levesy until a little while ago, Marshal. And I don't hire out my gun."

"You've got the look of it. Morgan, you said you're called . . ."

Cumberland glanced at the litter of papers on his desk.

"You can look through those reward dodgers all you want, Marshal, but you won't find any of them with my name on them," The Kid said.

"All right, don't get your back up. It's my job to keep the peace here."

"That includes letting Jed Ahern get away with murder?"

The chair let out a loud creak as Cumberland sat forward sharply. "You don't know what that bunch from the Broken Spoke is like! I'm sorry about Ed Phillips, damned sorry. He was a good man. Drove a freight wagon up here from the railroad every few weeks so we'd always have supplies on the shelves in the stores. And yeah, Ahern murdered him, no matter who threw the first punch or pulled a gun first. It was pure murder and we both know it."

"Then why—"

Cumberland stood up and paced across the room. "Because when Harlan Levesy hears I've got his foreman locked up in jail and charged with murder, he'll send his men to turn Ahern loose. And if I try to stop them, they'll kill me. And when they're done with killing me, they're liable to turn on the rest of the town. I don't think they'd burn it to the ground . . . Levesy needs a settlement of some sort here . . . but they'd go on a rampage . . . do a lot of damage and hurt some people. Probably kill some people, if you want the truth of it. So you tell me, Mr. Morgan . . . is justice for a man's life worth that price, especially when in the end there won't be any justice?"

The Kid returned the bleak stare Cumberland gave him. He didn't have an answer except some abstract nonsense about the kind of law and justice that didn't mean a damned thing in the face of an attack by a crew of kill-crazed gun-wolves.

After a moment Cumberland sighed. "Well, it's too late to do anything about it now. Ahern won't be in the mood to forgive being locked up like this. He'll have to have his vengeance on the town . . . and on you. You beat him, and for that he'll have to kill you. I suppose if you were to light a shuck out of here right now and be long gone by the time he got loose, he might not wreak too much havoc on the rest of us. Might even be that nobody else would die. But you can't ever tell with Ahern and the rest of that bunch." He paused, then added, "I don't suppose you'd leave town?"

"Run, you mean?"

"It might save some lives."

"This time. Maybe." The Kid shook his head. "Somebody needs to take the Broken Spoke down a notch."

"Yeah," Cumberland said bitterly. "That'd be a neat trick, now wouldn't it?"

The Kid went to the door and looked back at the marshal. "Are you going to let Ahern go as soon as I walk out of here?"

Cumberland shook his head. "No. Like I said, it's too late for that. What I'm going to do is ride out to the Broken Spoke and have a talk with Harlan Levesy. Plead with him to be reasonable. That probably won't do any good, either, but I'll try."

"Good luck, Marshal," The Kid said.

"I will need it," Cumberland said softly.

The Kid left the office and walked back around the corner to Main Street. Evening was coming on, and not many people were moving around. It was a quiet time of day anyway, but a nervous hush hung over the town, like the calm before a sudden thunderstorm, something these people who lived on the Kansas plains knew well.

This storm would take human form, though, in the shape of the hardcases who rode for Harlan Levesy.

The Kid's long legs carried him toward the Trailblazer Saloon. Somebody had already cleaned up the glass and nailed boards over the broken window, but warm yellow light spilled through the window on the other side of the entrance. The Kid pushed the bat wings aside and went in.

He would have bet the saloon was a lot more raucous on a normal evening. Only a low hum of conversation was punctuated by the clink of glass on glass as drinks were poured. That hum came to an abrupt end at the sight of him.

Constance was sitting at a large round table in the back of the room. Jared Tate was with her, and so was the white-mustached man who had spoken up to condemn Ahern earlier. Tate smiled and lifted a hand when he spotted The Kid, who started across the room toward them. The buzz of talk started up again.

Constance and the man with the mustache had glasses and were sharing a bottle of whiskey. A mug half full of beer sat in front of Tate. As The Kid pulled back an empty chair, Constance asked, "What'll you have, Mr. Morgan? Whatever it is, it's on the house. Seeing that big ape Ahern handed his needin's for a change is worth it."

"Don't you mean dooming the town to death and destruction?" The Kid asked. "That seems to be the marshal's assessment of what I've done."

Constance let out an unladylike snort. "No offense to my friend Bert, but his boy Riley sees the sky falling every time there's a cloud. He's always been that way. Jumpy, ready to think the worst."

Tate said, "Are you *sure* he's the marshal? I would have sworn I was. Riley Cumberland's not old enough to be a lawman."

Constance patted his hand. "We're all a heap older than it seems like we should be, Jared."

"I guess so. It's just that when I look around, there's so much that's not right. Just not right . . ."

"Did you get Ahern locked up all right?" The man with the mustache stuck out his hand. "I'm Milt Bennett, by the way. Own the livery stable."

"Kid Morgan," The Kid introduced himself as he shook hands with Bennett. "Yeah, Ahern's behind bars . . . for now."

Bennett frowned. "Riley's gonna let him loose

once it's good and dark, isn't he? He'll hope that'll do some good, but it won't."

The Kid shook his head. "I wondered about that, too, but he claims he's not planning to do any such thing. He's riding out to the Broken Spoke to talk to Harlan Levesy instead."

"Like that'll do any good." Constance pounded the table with her fist. "No, we're finally going to have to stand up to that bunch and let them know they can't waltz in here and do whatever they please. Once they see that, they'll back down. The town's just as important to Levesy as his business is to the town."

The Kid hoped she was right about that, but he had his doubts.

"You didn't tell me what you wanted to drink," Constance went on.

"Beer's fine," The Kid said. With trouble possibly on the way, it would be a good idea to keep a clear head.

Constance signaled to one of the bartenders, then added, "I'll have some food brought over, too. I imagine it's been a while since you and Jared ate."

"It has been," The Kid admitted. "Thanks."

Then, with a touch of the same bleakness that gripped Riley Cumberland, he thought, *And the condemned men ate a hearty last meal.*

Chapter 10

The food Constance had brought to the table was unusual fare for a saloon—sausages and cabbage—but good, The Kid thought, and he was hungry enough to enjoy it. While he and Tate were eating, Constance and Milt Bennett continued talking about how things had gone sour around Copperhead Springs ever since Cy Levesy died and left the Broken Spoke to his son.

"I think Cy knew Harlan wasn't much good, even though he didn't want to admit it," Bennett said. "He raised the boy by himself after his wife died when Harlan was mighty young. He wasn't cut out for it, though. He knew he'd done something wrong, but couldn't figure out how to fix it."

"A few good beatings might've gone a long way," Constance said caustically. "But I'm not sure even that would have helped Harlan."

"How many smaller spreads has Levesy taken over?" The Kid asked.

"Let's see." Bennett frowned in thought and counted on his fingers. "I make it four."

"That's right," Constance agreed with a nod. "They were all little greasy sack outfits that didn't amount to much . . . but even so, Harlan didn't have the right to run off their owners and gobble them up that way."

"Nobody's ever gone to the law about him? Sent for the county sheriff?"

"The county sheriff got a nice big campaign donation from Harlan in last year's election," Constance explained. "He's always going to find some excuse not to come over here and look into what's going on."

"How about wiring the governor, then?" The Kid suggested.

"The governor was good friends with Cy. He's not going to believe Cy's son is doing anything wrong. That would be disloyal to his old friend."

The Kid nodded slowly. From the sound of it, the people of Copperhead Springs were in a bad fix, all right. They couldn't look to outside help and weren't able to stand up to the men from the Broken Spoke on their own.

"I should do something about this," Tate declared with a determined frown. "I'm the marshal, and it's my job to see to it the laws are enforced."

"Oh, honey, you're not the marshal anymore," Constance told him. "I know you may not remember that, but it's true. We appreciate the sentiment, but it's not your job to help us."

"But if I'm not the marshal, then who is?"

"Riley Cumberland," Bennett said.

"That's not possible. He's a little boy."

Constance sighed. The Kid knew what she was

thinking. They'd had this conversation before with Tate. Not as far as Tate was concerned, though. It was all new to him.

"I hate to say it," Bennett said, "but maybe we need to go see Riley and ask him to release Ahern. It was easy to get carried away with the idea of standing up to the Broken Spoke, but if we do it's liable to be the town's ruination. Maybe if we let Ahern go now, he'll spare most of us."

Constance nodded toward The Kid. "What about Mr. Morgan here? You think Ahern's gonna just forget about settling the score with him?"

With a surly look on his face, Bennett said, "No offense, Mr. Morgan, but we have to think about the good of the town—"

"So I'll be the sacrificial goat," The Kid said with a wry smile.

"It's not that way, exactly—"

"You're hoping Ahern will kill me and leave the rest of you alone. I don't know what else you'd call it."

"Nobody's gonna be sacrificed," Constance said. "Milt, I'm surprised to hear you talk this way."

"Just trying to think about the good of the town," Bennett said again, but he looked down at the table, clearly embarrassed.

The talk continued aimlessly for a while before The Kid said, "I think I'll go back over to the jail and check on Marshal Cumberland."

"Make sure he hasn't already turned Ahern loose, you mean?" Constance asked.

"He said he was going out to the Broken Spoke to talk to Harlan Levesy. How long would that take?"

"The ranch headquarters is about an hour's ride from here," Bennett said. "Depending on when he left . . . if he left . . . he could be back pretty soon."

Tate got to his feet at the same time The Kid did. "I'll come with you. I may not be the marshal here anymore, although I still don't see how that's possible, but I know my way around the jail."

Constance said gently, "Why don't you stay here with me, Jared? It's been a long time since I've seen you, and I missed you, you know?"

The Kid looked at her and wondered if there had been any sort of romantic relationship between her and Tate. The two of them were about the same age, and evidently neither of them was married. They might have had to be discreet about it, what with him being the town marshal and her running a saloon, but it was possible. Whenever Constance looked at Tate, The Kid saw a gentleness and affection in her eyes that belied what seemed to be her usual hard-boiled attitude.

Tate responded to that as he moved around the table and put a hand on her shoulder. "I'll come back, Constance, don't worry about me. I just want to give The Kid a hand if he needs one."

She reached up, put her hand on his where it

rested on her shoulder, and squeezed. "All right. But be careful."

She gave The Kid a hard look. She was holding him responsible for Tate's safety.

He nodded slightly to show he understood. "Come on, Marshal."

They left the Trailblazer and started up the street toward the jail. Copperhead Springs really did appear to be deserted. Lights burned only in the saloon and a few other buildings, one of which was the marshal's office. Other than that, the town was dark and quiet as its citizens waited fearfully to see what was going to happen.

The Kid thought the door to the marshal's office might be locked, especially if Cumberland wasn't there, but it swung open easily when he twisted the knob. Cumberland wasn't in the office, although a lamp burned on the desk. Through the small, barred window set into the door between the office and the cell block, The Kid could see only darkness. Loud, obnoxious snoring came from one of the cells. Jed Ahern had gotten tired of cussing and gone to sleep.

Tate stood in the center of the room and looked around like a man who had come home after a long absence. "Are you sure I'm not the marshal anymore?"

"That's what everybody says," The Kid replied. "I don't think they're lying."

"It just . . . It seems like I belong here."

"I know what you mean," The Kid said.

If somehow all his memories of the past few years faded from his mind and he could walk back into the mansion in Carson City where Conrad Browning had lived with his wife Rebel, he would have felt like he was supposed to be there, too. As if somehow nothing had changed . . .

But it had changed. The mansion was gone, consumed by fire, and Rebel was dead. Conrad Browning was just a memory, too, and that was the way it had to be. The Kid's last attempt to reclaim his former life had ended in failure, and he would never allow himself to be trapped like that again.

Tate looked at the chair behind the desk. "You reckon he'd mind?"

"I wouldn't much care if he did." The Kid waved a hand at the chair. "Go ahead."

Tate sat down, took his hat off, and placed it on the desk. He leaned back in the chair with an expression of utter satisfaction on his face.

A swift rataplan of hoofbeats sounded in the street outside.

Something about the hoofbeats made The Kid stiffen as tension gripped him. His hand moved toward his gun as he turned to face the door, which he and Tate had left standing partially open. Shots blasted in the night.

The Kid twisted and blew out the lamp on the desk, plunging the office into darkness.

"Stay here!" he told Tate.

"But I'm the—"

"No, you're not! Stay here!"

The Kid drew his gun as he moved to the door and looked out. There had been only three shots, and as he peered toward Main Street, he saw a figure on horseback had come to a stop at the corner. He couldn't make out any details about the rider, but he felt confident the man was the one who had fired the shots.

The man shoved something from the back of his horse. It thudded to the ground. The rider whirled his mount and galloped off.

The shots had been to get everybody's attention, The Kid thought. It wasn't an attack. The man had been announcing that he was delivering some-thing.

The Kid had a bad feeling about what that something might be.

He opened the door and stepped out, and as he did he heard Tate moving behind him. He was about to tell the old lawman again to stay there, but changed his mind, figuring it would be all right for Tate to come along. His instincts told him for the moment there was no danger.

The two of them trotted toward whatever the horseman had dumped in the street. Up and down the blocks, the shots had drawn a few people out of the buildings, but nobody seemed anxious to investigate the commotion. As they got closer to the dark shape, The Kid recognized it as human, just as he'd feared.

He holstered his gun, reached into his pocket, and pulled out the metal container of matches that had saved his life a few days earlier. He shook one of the matches from the tin and snapped it to life as he knelt beside the man lying in the street.

Just as The Kid expected, the man was Marshal Riley Cumberland. It appeared he had gone out to the Broken Spoke just as he'd said he was going to.

He hadn't gotten a warm welcome, though. His face was swollen, bruised, and smeared with blood from numerous cuts and scrapes. His clothes were tattered and torn, and from the looks of them, as well as the damage to Cumberland's body, he had been tied behind a horse and dragged over rough ground.

But at least he was alive. Ragged breaths rasped in his throat. That was a little more than The Kid had expected. He'd thought they would find Cumberland dead when they reached his side.

"Good Lord," Tate muttered. "Poor hombre's been beaten within an inch of his life. I'll have to find out who did this."

"We know who—" The Kid began, then stopped. Explaining things to Tate would be a waste of time and breath. "He needs help. A doctor."

"Doc Franklin," Tate said without hesitation. "His office isn't far from here."

Given the source, that might be true, or it might not.

A woman's voice called, "What is it? Who's there?"

The Kid glanced up to see Constance coming down the street toward them, a lantern in her upraised hand. Bennett was with her, along with several other men, and a couple were armed with shotguns.

The swamper Bert, Riley Cumberland's father, was with the group as well. He cried out and rushed forward. "Riley! My God, Riley! What have they done?"

Bert dropped to his knees beside the unconscious marshal, lifted Cumberland's head, and cradled it in his lap.

The Kid got to his feet and turned to meet the others.

"Sorry it took us a few minutes to get here. I'll be honest, we had to talk ourselves into it. We didn't know what we'd find out here." Constance glanced at Cumberland and lowered her voice. "Is he dead?"

The Kid shook his head. "No, but he needs a doctor. Marshal Tate mentioned a Doc Franklin . . ."

"Yeah, he's still here, the only doctor we have." Constance turned to the men with her and issued orders in a familiar tone of command. "Some of you boys pick him up and take him to the doc's house. And be careful with him! There's no telling how bad he's busted up inside."

Bert didn't want to let go of his son, but the men gently worked Cumberland's unconscious form away from him. They lifted Cumberland and carried him to a side street with the rest of the group following.

A man in a nightshirt and robe met them on the porch of a small, neat house. He had gray hair and a broad, florid face. "When I heard the shots I knew I'd likely be needed, so I got up and got ready. Take him into the first room there." The doctor shook his head in dismay as he looked at Cumberland and echoed Tate's comment. "Good Lord."

The Kid, Tate, Constance, and Milt Bennett stepped back out onto the porch.

Constance said, "I could've told Riley he couldn't talk any sense into Harlan Levesy. He was just wasting his time. He's lucky that bunch didn't kill him."

The Kid shook his head. "Levesy didn't want to kill the marshal. He wanted him left alive for a reason . . . to send a message to the rest of you here in town."

"That message being that we can expect the same or worse from the Broken Spoke?" Constance asked harshly.

The Kid nodded. "That's right. The only question is when."

Chapter 11

It was close to an hour before the doctor came out onto the porch to report that Riley Cumberland was still alive and had in fact regained consciousness.

Most of the men had drifted away, going back to the saloon or to their homes. The Kid, Constance, Tate, and Bennett were still there, as was Bert, who sat in a wicker rocking chair rocking back and forth slightly.

When Franklin delivered his news, Bert jumped up from the chair. "Then he's going to be all right, Doc?"

"I didn't say that," Franklin cautioned. "He's been through a lot, been treated mighty rough. I think he'll recover, but he'll need a lot of rest." The doctor frowned. "He ought to be asleep now, but he's insisting he talk to you, Mr. Morgan."

"Me?" The Kid said, surprised. It seemed to him if Cumberland talked to anyone, it ought to be Bert, his own father.

"That's what he said. But if you're going to do it, it ought to be soon. I'm not sure how long he'll be awake."

"Go ahead, Mr. Morgan," Constance urged. "It could be something important."

The Kid supposed she was right. He nodded

to the doctor, who led him into the house.

Riley Cumberland was lying in bed, propped up with several pillows. His eyes were closed, and his face was pale and drawn in the lamplight. Doc Franklin had bandaged the worst of the cuts, but Cumberland's features were still swollen and bruised.

His eyes opened slowly at the sound of foot-steps from the two men. He seemed to have a little trouble, but after a moment he was able to focus on The Kid. "M-Morgan."

"I'm here, Marshal. What can I do for you?"

"I can tell . . . from that ruckus with Ahern . . . that you're a fighting man," Cumberland whispered. "You're the only one . . . who can help these folks. Levesy said . . . he and his men are coming to town . . . at sunup tomorrow."

"To turn Ahern loose?" The Kid guessed.

"Yeah." Cumberland licked his lips. "Doc, can I . . . get a drink?"

"Water," Franklin said. "That's all."

"That'll . . . do."

Franklin took a cup from the bedside table and lifted it to Cumberland's mouth. The marshal took a sip, spilling some of the water but getting some of it down his throat. That seemed to strengthen him slightly.

"Harlan said to have Ahern waiting for them . . . said if he wasn't turned loose by then, they'd take him out of the jail . . . and make the town pay for defying him. Give him what he wants, and he promised . . . they wouldn't kill anybody."

"Is that all?"

Cumberland's head moved slightly from side to side. "No . . . He heard about how you . . . beat Ahern. The town has to . . . turn you over to them as well."

"And if that doesn't happen?"

"He said that Broken Spoke . . . would make everybody in Copperhead Springs sorry."

"Did he tell you all this before or after they tied you to a horse and dragged you?"

A little croaking sound came from Cumberland. It took The Kid a moment to realize the marshal was laughing.

"Harlan said all that . . . before his boys jumped me. Said for me to . . . see that what he wanted was done."

"What did you tell him?" The Kid asked.

Again that croaking laughter. "Told him . . . to go to hell."

Having seen what he had of Marshal Riley Cumberland, The Kid wouldn't have thought the lawman had that much defiance in him. But the marshal's badly beaten condition seemed to indicate he was telling the truth.

"He told his men . . . to be sure not to kill me," Cumberland went on. "He wanted me alive . . . to bring his message back to town."

That agreed with the theory The Kid had

explained to Constance earlier. "So what is it you want me to do, Marshal? Do you really expect me to turn Ahern loose and surrender myself to Levesy's men?"

"No . . . Hell, no . . . Got to . . . fight them. Get everybody together . . . tell them it's time to fight . . ."

"If I do that," The Kid warned, "innocent people are liable to get hurt."

"You think they won't get hurt . . . if the Broken Spoke keeps running things . . . around here?"

Cumberland had a point there, The Kid thought. Innocent people like Ed Phillips had already been hurt. And others would continue to suffer at the hands of the Broken Spoke crew as long as they were a law unto themselves.

"That's enough," Franklin said. "He really has to rest now."

"Not yet!" Cumberland tried to push himself up from the pillows, but grimaced as he failed. "Give me . . . your word, Morgan."

"I can't speak for anybody else in town," The Kid said, "but I don't like giving in to skunks like that. I won't back up from their trouble."

"Good," Cumberland breathed. "People will look at you . . . and know what they need to do."

The Kid never set out to be anybody's leader. Sometimes circumstances thrust him into that role, however, and it appeared to be one of those times, he thought as Cumberland's eyes closed.

The battered lawman's chest rose and fell fairly steadily as sleep claimed him.

"He's worn out," Franklin said quietly. "Be the best thing in the world for him if he sleeps the clock around."

"Maybe," The Kid said. "Question is, if he does that will there still be a town here when he wakes up?"

He left the doctor and the marshal and returned to the front porch.

Bert clutched at The Kid's sleeve. "How is he? What did he have to say? Is he going to be all right?"

The others gathered around The Kid to hear what he'd learned. "I'm no sawbones, but I think the marshal will recover. He's resting now. I'm sorry you didn't get a chance to talk to him, Bert."

The swamper sighed and shook his head. "As long as he's all right, it don't really matter. It's, uh, not like he ever talks that much to me anyway."

"Why did he want to talk to you, Mr. Morgan?" Constance asked.

"To pass on a warning. Harlan Levesy's riding to town with his men the first thing in the morning. He expects Ahern to be turned loose by then, or he'll take it out on the town."

"What'd I tell you?" Bennett said. "That's what we have to do."

Constance looked at The Kid. "That's not all Levesy wants, is it?"

"Well, no," The Kid replied with a faint smile. "He wants me, too. I expect he wants to turn me over to Ahern."

"So Ahern can kill you," Constance said heavily.

"I'm not afraid of Ahern."

"Maybe not, but I say no! We don't turn Ahern loose, and we sure as hell don't serve you up on a silver platter."

"You'd better think about that, Constance," Bennett urged. "We never even saw this man before today."

"I don't care. I'm not gonna condemn him to death just because I'm afraid of Harlan Levesy." The woman's voice was scornful as she added, "And I'm a little surprised and disappointed that you would, Milt."

"I've got a family and a business to think about," Bennett snapped. "Those things have to come first."

"What if Harlan Levesy decides he wants to take over that business one of these days? What if he comes to you, offers you a fraction of what the stable's worth and tells you you'd better accept . . . or else?"

"Why would he do that? He's not interested in taking over anything here in town."

"Not yet, maybe," Constance replied. "But I never yet saw a man hungry for power who was willing to back away from the table."

The Kid thought she was right about that.

Her words appeared to have gotten through to Bennett, too, as he stood frowning and looking uncertain. After a moment he said, "If we don't give in, what *can* we do?"

"Fight," Constance answered without hesitation.

"That's what Marshal Cumberland wanted me to do," The Kid offered. "He asked me to get folks together and get them ready to take on the Broken Spoke."

"But those men who work for Levesy are killers!" Bennett objected. "We're just . . . just normal people."

"You can hold a gun, point it, and shoot it, can't you?" Constance asked.

"Yeah, and I can get shot, too!"

"A horse could kick you in the head and kill you tomorrow, Milt. You just don't know. None of us do. We risk our lives every time we get up in the morning. Wouldn't it be a good idea to risk them for something worthwhile for a change?"

The Kid was willing to let Constance do most of the talking. She was good at it. He had other talents, most of which involved killing.

Those would be needed, too, before it was over.

"All right," Bennett said. "I don't like being run roughshod over any more than you do. And it's true there's no telling what Levesy will do in the future if we don't stop him now. If we back down from him—again!—it'll convince him he can do whatever he damn well pleases and get away with it."

"That's the spirit," Constance said with a curt nod. She turned to The Kid. "It appears the marshal put you in charge, Mr. Morgan. What do we do now?"

"Spread the word. Anybody who has a gun and is willing to fight needs to be somewhere downtown at sunup tomorrow. That's where we'll make our stand. Anybody who's not going to fight needs to lay as low as possible. We don't want to have to worry about them."

"Where will you be?"

"I plan on being front and center," The Kid said. "I think it'll be time for Harlan Levesy and me to meet face-to-face."

<u>Chapter 12</u>

With the showdown coming first thing in the morning, The Kid knew he needed some rest. While Constance and Bennett split up to spread the word through Copperhead Springs, The Kid and Jared Tate returned to the marshal's office. There was an old sofa in the office where The Kid figured he could stretch out and get a little sleep.

Tate had been quiet during the discussion of how to meet the threat from the Broken Spoke, but when they reached the office, he said, "I wish Cy Levesy was still alive. I can't believe he isn't. He'd put a stop to this in a hurry."

"I'm sure he would, Marshal."

"You don't have to call me that," Tate said with a shake of his head. He looked down at the badge pinned to his vest. "I know this tin star of mine is just an old souvenir."

"You wore it proudly. No reason you still can't."

"I appreciate that." Tate sat down behind the desk. "Hard to believe little Riley Cumberland grew up to be the marshal. He was always getting in trouble when he was a kid. No ma to raise him, you know, just Bert. And Bert was always either drunk or working at some odd job to make money for whiskey. Riley . . . well, Riley always sort of hated his old man, I think."

"Bert cares about him," The Kid said.

"Yeah. A father always does. Why, I always doted on my girl Bertha." Tate smiled. "I remember last year I brought this puppy home for her . . ." His voice trailed away. After a moment he said, "That wasn't last year, was it?"

"Probably not," The Kid said.

"She's a grown woman now. Got a husband and kids of her own. I . . . I seem to recall staying with them for a spell . . ."

"I'm sure you'll go back and see them when this trouble is all over," The Kid said.

He hadn't given much thought to what should be done about Tate, but clearly he needed somebody looking after him. He couldn't be left alone to roam around on his own, lost in the past with his memories going in and out of his head.

The Kid stretched out on the sofa and tipped his hat down over his eyes. "I'm going to get some shut-eye. But I'll be awake in time to get ready for Levesy and the bunch from the Broken Spoke. You won't wander off, will you, Marshal?"

"No, I'll stay right here," Tate declared firmly. "Don't worry, Kid, I'll hold down the fort."

Like most frontiersmen, The Kid had developed the knack of being able to go to sleep quickly and wake up when he wanted to. He dozed off almost as soon as he closed his eyes, and when he opened them he knew it was about an hour before dawn.

The marshal's office was dark. The lamp had either gone out, or Tate had turned it out. The Kid sat up on the sofa. "Marshal?"

No one answered him.

He swung his legs off the old sofa and stood up. He had spent enough time in the marshal's office that he sort of knew where things were, so he was able to cross the room and find the desk. He took the glass chimney off the lamp, struck a match, and lit the wick. The yellow glow that welled up revealed the room was empty except for The Kid.

He bit back a curse. He had told Tate not to wander off!

And he had trusted a man whose mind was half gone to do what he was told. It was his own fault,

The Kid thought. He had never before dealt with anyone who had the sort of problems Tate did, and he had made assumptions he shouldn't have made.

It was too late to do anything except look for the old lawman . . . and he had to get out and see how the town was progressing with its preparations for the Broken Spoke crew, he reminded himself. He could combine those two tasks.

Leaving the lamp burning in case Tate came back, The Kid left the marshal's office and went to the corner. The buildings along Main Street were dark, but as he started along the boardwalk, someone called softly, "Who's that?"

"Morgan," The Kid replied.

An audible sigh of relief came from the man who had challenged him. "Constance said you were takin' over as the marshal, Mr. Morgan." The man stepped out of the dark mouth of an alley, holding a rifle slanted across his chest. "Do you have any orders?"

The Kid started to explain he wasn't the marshal, or even an acting lawman, but there didn't seem to be any point. "Do you know where the other men are set up?"

"Not all of 'em, no, but I got a couple fellas in this alley with me, and I know there's a man with a rifle on top of the hardware store across the street."

"That's good," The Kid said with a nod.

"Uh, Marshal . . . when the Broken Spoke gets

here, how will we know if we're supposed to start shootin'?"

A grim chuckle came from The Kid. "You'll know. You haven't seen Marshal Tate, have you?"

"The old fella who used to be the marshal here? No, can't say as I have."

"Well, if you see him, tell him to go back to the marshal's office, will you?"

"Sure thing, Mr. Morgan."

The Kid moved on up the street and encountered men barricaded inside stores, crouched behind water barrels, and waiting behind false fronts. When he spoke to them, he heard the tension in their voices, but at least they seemed to have their nerves under control.

No one had seen Jared Tate. It was possible the old lawman had found himself a saddled horse, mounted up, and ridden off bound for no telling what destination. *In a way that would be better,* The Kid thought. Tate would be well out of harm's way, at least as far as the potential battle with Levesy's men. Of course, he might find himself in other danger.

When The Kid reached the Trailblazer Saloon, he found Constance sitting on a bench in front of the saloon with a shotgun across her knees. "The town's ready. As ready as it's ever going to be, I guess."

The Kid nodded. "I'd say we've got between

thirty and forty men waiting to join in when the shooting starts."

"Don't you mean *if* the shooting starts?" Constance asked with wry humor.

"I'd like to think there's a chance of that, but from everything I've heard about Harlan Levesy, that's not what I'm expecting."

"And you'd be wise not to," Constance agreed. "He won't back down. I never saw a man with more stubborn pride in my life. Reckon it comes from feeling like he could never measure up to his father."

"Do you know how many men he has in his crew?"

"That depends on whether he brings all his hands or just the gunnies. He has about ten actual cowboys working for him, taking care of the real work on the Broken Spoke, but twenty hombres who were hired for their guns."

"So we'll outnumber them either way."

"Yeah," Constance said, "assuming none of our men lose their nerve and run. And you've got to remember that a professional killer is more than a match for two or three store clerks and black-smiths."

The Kid knew that, but it was too late to worry about such considerations. He changed the subject. "Have you seen Marshal Tate?"

"Jared?" Constance sat up straighter and peered sharply at The Kid in the gray predawn light. "Blast it, you haven't lost him, have you?"

"He was in the marshal's office when I dozed off for a while, but when I woke up . . ."

"Damn it! I should have kept him with me."

"I'm sorry," The Kid said. "I didn't think about him wandering off like that, and I should have."

"He wandered off from his daughter's house in Wichita and wound up here, clear across the state. There's no telling where he might go."

The Kid didn't mention he'd already thought that same thing.

"Well, he's bound to be around somewhere. As long as he stays out of the line of fire, we can always find him later," Constance went on. "Assuming there is a later."

"I got the feeling that at one time the two of you—"

"Mind your own business," she broke in. "What happened a long time ago doesn't have anything to do with what happens today."

"The past always has an effect on the present," The Kid said, thinking about all the times his own past had risen up to torment him.

"I guess so, but we've got bigger worries right now, like surviving the next hour."

He nodded. "You'd better go inside and stay there."

She lifted the shotgun. "I didn't bring this Greener out here for show."

102

"No, but you can shoot over the bat wings if you need to, or from a window."

"Maybe, but it'll be another half hour before the Broken Spoke gets here." She took a deep breath. "I'm enjoying the morning air."

The Kid didn't waste time arguing with her. He just nodded and brought up something that had occurred to him. "When I ran into Marshal Tate, he told me he was on his way back from delivering a prisoner to Fort Hays. Somebody named Brick Cantrell."

Constance nodded. "Jared took Cantrell to the army, all right . . . ten years ago."

"So that part was true."

"You bet it was. Cantrell was a real bad hombre. Deserted from the army and put together a gang that rampaged all over this part of the country. After they raided the town, Jared put together a posse and went after them. They managed to catch the gang napping and jumped them. Killed about half the owlhoots, and the other half got away . . . except for Cantrell. They captured him and brought him back, and Jared turned him over to the army. He's been locked up ever since." Constance sighed. "Yeah, in his time, Jared Tate was one hell of a lawman, to put it bluntly. And now we have to worry about him because he might have wandered off and doesn't know where he is. It's just sad."

The Kid agreed. He nodded and moved on to

check the defenders ranged along the rest of the street.

A golden glow had started to creep into the eastern sky, spreading like water flowing across the heavens. While he still had a little time, The Kid went back to the marshal's office, thinking Tate might have returned there out of habit, but the room was still empty.

He went to the cell block door and opened it. Jed Ahern wasn't sleeping and snoring anymore. The huge, ape-like man stood at the door of his cell, his fingers wrapped around the iron bars. "Where's the marshal?" he demanded. "He better let me outta here if he knows what's good for him."

"Marshal Cumberland can't do anything right now," The Kid said. "He went out to the Broken Spoke yesterday evening to try to talk sense to your boss."

A vicious grin spread across Ahern's face. "So he's dead, is he?"

"No, but no thanks to Levesy and the rest of that bunch."

"Well, he'll be dead soon enough," Ahern said with callous disregard. "And so will you, mister. If I know Harlan, him and the boys will be showin' up any time to teach this town a lesson it'll never forget."

"Maybe they'll try," The Kid said. "Maybe they'll find that the citizens have more backbone than you're giving them credit for."

Ahern let out a disgusted snort. "Yeah, sure. Some of 'em might talk big, but they'll fall over and piss themselves like scared dogs if a real man even looks hard at 'em. If you're countin' on them to put up a fight, you're about to find out what it's like to be all by yourself facin' mighty tall odds."

The Kid hoped Ahern was wrong and it wouldn't turn out that way. He wouldn't know how the townspeople would react until the time to fight actually arrived.

And that time was coming soon, he realized as he glanced out the cell's window and saw the orange glow in the sky. The sun was almost up.

He turned, walked out of the cell block, and locked the door behind him, ignoring Ahern's harsh laughter following him. He left the marshal's office and walked the half block to Main Street as the dawn light grew brighter around him. A glance to the east showed the brilliant orb of the sun just starting to poke above the horizon.

And from the west suddenly came the thunder of hoofbeats. The Kid walked out into the middle of Main Street to meet the men of the Broken Spoke.

Chapter 13

Dust boiled up from the hooves of the horses charging toward the settlement. The Kid glanced along the street. He saw men here and there, peering nervously out from the spots where they had taken cover.

The Kid knew he was taking a chance, meeting Harlan Levesy out in the open. He was counting on the man's pride and arrogance to keep him from ordering an immediate attack. Levesy would want to confront the man who dared to challenge him.

That appeared to be the case. As the riders entered the western end of the street, the man in the lead held up a hand, signaling them to a stop. The dust swirled around them for a moment, obscuring The Kid's view, but as it began to drift away he was able to see there were about twenty men in the group.

Levesy had left his regular ranch hands on the Broken Spoke. Clearly, he didn't think he would need them to impose his will on the town.

The leader walked his horse out a few yards ahead of the others. He wore an expensive tan jacket and Stetson. As far as The Kid could tell, he wasn't armed.

That came as no surprise. Levesy would be the

sort to rely on others doing his shooting for him.

One of the other men spoke to him. Levesy turned his head and replied, then moved his hand in a curt gesture. The others stayed where they were as Levesy walked his horse toward The Kid.

When about twenty feet separated them, Levesy reined his mount to a halt again. He was a young man, around twenty-five, and darkly handsome with crisp black hair under his hat. He gave The Kid a smug smile and asked, "Who are you?"

"Name's Morgan," The Kid replied.

"Ah, you're the one who attacked my foreman."

"After he killed a man for no good reason."

Levesy shrugged. "That's your version of the story. I'm sure Jed will tell it differently. Bring him out here."

The Kid shook his head. "Ahern is in jail, and that's where he's going to stay until a judge says otherwise."

"Do you honestly think I can't get a judge to drop any charges against him and order him released?"

"I'm sure you can. You've probably got a judge or two in your pocket."

Levesy smiled and shrugged. The cruel arrogance that came with money and power fairly oozed from him.

He didn't know he was facing someone who, in another lifetime, could have bought and sold him at least a hundred times over. When it came to money and influence, even a successful rancher like Levesy couldn't approach Conrad Browning.

"The problem is, that would take too long," Levesy said. "I need Ahern released now. There's work waiting for him on the Broken Spoke. So go turn him loose, if you've taken over as the marshal for the time being, and we can be done with this."

"You'd take Ahern and go back to your ranch and not cause any problems for the town?"

"Well . . . my men are pretty upset that he was arrested in the first place. They might want to blow off a little steam. But not too much. I'd see to that."

"So they'd just bust up a few businesses, beat up a few citizens, and call it good? Is that it?"

Levesy's smug smile went away and his voice hardened. "You'd better take the best deal you can get, mister. Oh, and as for you . . . you'll be coming with us, too. I'm sure Jed will want to talk to you some more."

"He'd like to talk me right into a shallow grave out on the prairie."

"You shouldn't have butted in on something that wasn't any of your business," Levesy snapped. "My men do what they want, and that's just the way it is around here."

The Kid shook his head. "Not anymore."

"You're going to stop us?" Levesy flung out a hand in disbelief. "One man?"

"Look along the street," The Kid said quietly. "There are more than a dozen rifles pointed at you right now."

Levesy's eyes narrowed, and as he glanced along the street, The Kid saw uncertainty in his eyes for the first time.

That reaction didn't last long. Levesy shook his head in obvious disgust. "They won't shoot. They know if they do, I'll burn this town to the ground. I can always start over and build another town, one where the citizens are more . . . agreeable."

"You can't build anything if you're dead," The Kid said.

Levesy's nostrils flared. "You're threatening me? Me, personally?"

"You were the one who was a big enough damned fool to ride up here by yourself." The Kid gave a faint smile.

Levesy realized he had walked right into a trap. Anger reddened his face. "You can't shoot me. I'm unarmed. And if you did, my men would fill you full of lead before I hit the ground."

"Here's the thing," The Kid said. "If I'm going to die anyway, like you said, then I don't give a damn if you're unarmed. All I care about is that you go through Hell's swinging doors before I do."

Levesy's eyes widened. "You . . . you're crazy!"

"And you're going to be dead in about ten seconds if you don't order your men to go back to the ranch and stay there."

"You think we're going to just turn around and leave?"

"Nope," The Kid said. "They are. You're going to stay here. And I'd say you're down to about five seconds now."

Levesy's eyes widened until it seemed they were about to pop out of their sockets. He swallowed hard. "You mean it."

"I do. And time's up." It was a bluff . . . probably. The Kid disliked Harlan Levesy enough he might have considered shooting the man. But he didn't think he'd have to.

And he was right. Levesy twisted in his saddle to look back at his men and bellowed, "Go back to the ranch! Now!"

The gunmen hadn't been able to hear the conversation between their boss and the stranger standing so casually in the middle of the street. Their horses moved around a little as they tried to figure out if they should obey the command.

"Do it!" Levesy shouted.

"What about Jed, boss?" asked the man who had spoken to Levesy earlier.

"We'll worry about Jed later," Levesy snapped.

"Now you're being smart," The Kid said.

Levesy gave him a glance dripping with hate. "You're going to be sorry about this, Morgan. More sorry than you can dream of."

The Kid ignored that. "Get down from that horse."

Levesy dismounted as his men turned their horses and started to leave Copperhead Springs. He dropped the reins and asked, "What are you going to do, put me in jail with Ahern?"

"That's what I was thinking—"

Levesy didn't give him time to finish, launching himself in a diving tackle that drove The Kid off his feet. That act of personal violence was something he hadn't expected at all.

But he wasn't surprised when Levesy started hammering punches at him and yelled to the hired guns, "Burn the town! Burn it to the ground!"

With shouts of excitement, the men from the Broken Spoke whirled their horses, yanked guns from holsters, and charged forward. It looked like they were going to have some fun after all.

The gunmen began to rake the fronts of the buildings with a storm of lead. The defenders returned the fire. The Kid heard shots roaring all around him, but didn't have time to see how the battle was going. He had his hands full with Harlan Levesy, who was turning out to be a surprisingly tough opponent.

Levesy might be spoiled, rich, and arrogant, but he could fight. Several blows rocked The Kid's head back and forth before he got his arms up to block them. He shot a left into the face of the man pinning him to the ground. The blow jolted Levesy's head back but didn't dislodge him from his superior position. He dug a knee into

111

The Kid's belly, making it hard for him to breathe.

The Kid got his hands on the lapels of Levesy's expensive jacket, bunched his fingers in the material, and heaved hard to the side, sending Levesy rolling through the dust.

His gunmen weren't shooting toward the middle of the street where their boss was, but one of them had to swerve his charging horse aside to avoid trampling Levesy. Bullets coming from both sides of the street zipped through the air. The Kid knew he was in as much danger of being hit by a shot fired by one of the defenders as he was from Levesy's men.

He lunged after Levesy and swung a fist, landing the blow so solidly it seemed for a second Levesy's head was going to turn all the way around on his neck. The punch knocked him senseless. The Kid scooped him up, draped him over a shoulder, and made a run for the Trailblazer Saloon.

"He's got the boss!" one of the hired killers shouted. "Get him!"

Hoofbeats thundered right behind The Kid as a couple men closed in on him.

Constance stepped out through the bat wings and yelled, "Get down, Morgan!" as she pointed her shotgun at the pursuers.

The Kid hit the dirt in front of the boardwalk as Constance touched off both barrels. The double charge of buckshot erupted from the shotgun

112

with a roar like doomsday and swept both gunmen from their saddles.

The Kid surged to his feet, taking Levesy with him, and charged up the steps to the saloon. Constance held the bat wings aside for him as he carried Levesy into the building. Dumping the young rancher unceremoniously on the sawdust-littered floor, The Kid panted, "Keep . . . an eye on him!"

"You can count on that," Constance promised as she snapped the scattergun closed after sliding two fresh shells into it.

The Kid turned back toward the door and drew his Colt. The battle for Copperhead Springs wasn't over yet.

Chapter 14

Levesy's men had come to town prepared, The Kid saw as he looked over the bat wings. While most of the gunmen traded shots with the defenders, several of them brought out torches— lengths of cloth soaked in kerosene and wrapped around pieces of wood.

With torches blazing brightly, the riders got ready to throw them at various buildings while their friends covered them.

The Kid stepped out onto the boardwalk and snapped a couple shots at a man charging toward

Milt Bennett's livery stable with a torch in his hand. The range was pretty far for a handgun, but luck and skill guided The Kid's shots. The slugs ripped through the gunman's body and knocked him out of the saddle. The torch fell in the street beside him, burning out harmlessly in the dust.

About to line up a shot on another torch-wielder, a more immediate threat lunged at The Kid. The form of a mounted gunman rode up emptying a Colt at him. He threw himself to the planks as bullets whined around his ears.

Slugs chewed splinters from the boardwalk as he came to a stop on his belly, angled his gun up, and sent a bullet through the gunman's throat. Blood from the wound fountained in the air as the man went backward out of the saddle.

The Kid got to his feet. The porch in front of one of the stores was already burning. A water barrel stood on the porch, and he quickly put two shots through it. Water spouted from the holes left by the bullets and spread across the porch. That might not put out all the flames, but at least it would slow them down.

With his gun empty, he ran to the corner of the saloon and crouched there while he reloaded, filling all six chambers. More splinters rained down on him as bullets hit the building above his head. He snapped the Colt's cylinder closed and brought it up to blow another of the gunmen off his horse.

Another rider raced by brandishing a torch. He never saw The Kid, and that was his bad luck. His head jerked as a bullet from The Kid's gun bored through his brain. The dead man and the torch he'd been carrying hit the ground at the same time.

A fierce gun battle was taking place in the next block as several of Levesy's men tried to overrun the townsmen who had taken cover behind a water trough. The defenders were about to be flanked, and as soon as that happened it would be easy for the killers to cut them down.

The Kid ran along the street, heedless of the bullets flying every which way, and shouted, "Hey!" as the gunmen closed in on the defenders.

He emptied the wheel—four remaining rounds —in the space of no more than two heartbeats, and four would-be killers went spinning off their feet with The Kid's lead in them.

That left him with an empty gun and no time to reload as another rider charged at him, firing as he came. The Kid leaped aside, and spotted Jared Tate suddenly step out from an alley.

The gun in the old lawman's hand roared and bucked, and the hired killer doubled over as a bullet punched into his belly. He didn't fall off the horse, but remained doubled over in agony as the animal raced away.

The Kid scrambled to his feet and nodded to Tate. "Much obliged, Marshal," he said as he quickly reloaded the Colt. "You've saved my life again."

"Glad to do it," Tate said. "Where's Cantrell? Let's get that damn scumdog!"

Tate thought he was fighting Brick Cantrell's gang again. Under the circumstances it didn't matter, but The Kid didn't want Tate getting too confused and start shooting innocent citizens. "Come on, Marshal! Let's head back to the Trailblazer! We'll make our stand there!"

"Lead the way, Deputy," Tate snapped.

So I'm a deputy now, The Kid thought. For all intents and purposes, he supposed he really was.

With Tate at his side, he raced toward the saloon. Gunmen charged them from both directions. The Kid and Tate fired right and left, battling their way through. By the time they reached the Trailblazer, only a few of Levesy's men were left to fight.

They charged the saloon in a last ditch attack.

The Kid and Tate swung around to meet them. The Kid dropped to one knee in front of the steps, Tate stood tall beside him, and Constance stepped out of the saloon with her shotgun to join them. Their guns roared and blasted, and the remaining killers went down in a welter of flailing hooves and shredded flesh.

Constance came down the steps, sliding fresh shells into the shotgun's chambers. "Is that all of them? Is it over?"

"We got 'em, all right," Tate said with a big grin on his weathered face. He turned to Constance, taking her by surprise as he put an arm around her shoulders and planted a kiss on her mouth.

"Why, you . . . you old geezer!" she said breathlessly as he stepped back a moment later. Then she let the shotgun slip to the ground as she put both hands on Tate's face and pulled him closer. "C'mere!"

The Kid chuckled as he turned away to let them share their moment.

He thumbed fresh cartridges into his revolver and looked along the street. All the outlaws were down, although some were still alive and moaning in pain. Smoke came from a couple buildings, but the townspeople were already fighting those blazes. He thought they stood a good chance of bringing the flames under control.

He wondered how many of the citizens had been killed in the fighting. It was a foregone conclusion the people of Copperhead Springs hadn't escaped without any casualties. The question was how bad the tragedy had turned out to be.

An incoherent shout made him spin around just as he pouched his iron. Having regained consciousness, Harlan Levesy burst out of the saloon with a gun in his hand. His face was contorted with hatred as he thrust the weapon at The Kid and pulled the trigger. Flame gouted from the pistol's muzzle.

Levesy was too crazed to aim properly. Marshal Tate grunted in pain and staggered as Constance cried, "Jared! No!"

The Kid didn't waste any time. Palming the Colt out again, he fired from the hip, triggering two shots that smashed into Levesy's chest. The impact made him take a step backward, although he didn't go down right away. Blood welled from his mouth as he struggled to lift the gun in his hand and get off another shot.

The Kid fired a third shot, and a black-rimmed hole appeared in the center of Levesy's forehead. He went down hard and didn't move again.

The Kid swung around to see Constance on her knees beside Tate's fallen form. Tears ran down her face.

Tate opened his eyes and said in a weak voice, "Constance? Constance, what's wrong? Why are you crying?"

"Because you're shot, you damned old fool!" she cried.

"Is that all?" Tate asked with a smile. "I've been shot before, you know."

His eyelids slid closed, but the smile remained on his face.

"He'll be fine," Doc Franklin assured The Kid, Constance, and all the other people gathered in his front room. "The bullet nicked him in the side, that's all. In a man his age, any bullet wound can be dangerous, but it's my professional opinion he'll be back on his feet in a few days."

Constance heaved a sigh of relief. "That's mighty good to know, Doc. I was afraid the old coot had gone and gotten himself killed."

"No, he should be all right. Unfortunately I can't say the same for half a dozen other citizens."

An air of sorrow mitigated the relief they felt over Marshal Jared Tate's condition. People had died during the battle, including Milt Bennett. People who had seen him go down with a smoking gun in his hand said that despite his reservations about putting up a fight, the liveryman had battled as valiantly as anyone and personally accounted for a couple hired killers before he fell.

The others who had died would be mourned, too, and no one would forget the sacrifice they had made to help free the town from the tyrannical grip of the Broken Spoke gunmen . . . but that wouldn't bring them back.

The Kid and Constance went into the room where Marshal Riley Cumberland lay recuperating. His father Bert was with him, sitting beside the bed with his hands clasped together anxiously.

When Cumberland heard them come in, his eyes fluttered open. "It's . . . it's all over then, is it?"

"That's right," Constance said. "Harlan Levesy is dead, and so are most of his gunnies."

Cumberland shook his head. "There's going to

119

be . . . a lot of trouble . . . over this. Levesy had . . . plenty of friends . . . in high places."

"I have a friend who knows some important folks, too," The Kid said, thinking of his lawyer Claudius Turnbuckle.

Turnbuckle could bring pressure to bear all the way to the corridors of power in Washington. The Kid was confident if he threw Conrad Browning's wealth and influence behind the citizens of Copperhead Springs, he could assure a fair and impartial investigation into the bloody affair. No one should suffer because they had finally risen up and defended themselves from Harlan Levesy and his hired killers.

And before it was all over, The Kid thought there was a good chance Jed Ahern would be convicted of murder and sentenced to hang. "I'll send some wires. We'll see to it the truth comes out."

He and Constance talked to Cumberland for a short time longer, then left to let the wounded marshal get some rest. As they walked back toward the Trailblazer, The Kid realized it was only mid-morning. That seemed impossible, considering how much had already happened.

"What are your plans once everything has settled down, Kid?" Constance asked.

"I don't know," he replied honestly. "I started in this direction thinking I might get a riding job, but that idea has sort of lost its appeal. Jared said he could get me a job at the Broken Spoke, but I've got a hunch whoever inherits it won't want to take me on."

"Probably not," Constance agreed. "Cy had a cousin back in Salina. I guess he'll get the spread now. Lord knows what he'll do with it. Probably sell it."

"I didn't set out to kill Levesy. I thought maybe I could head off the trouble somehow."

Constance shook her head. "You never had a chance in Hades of doing that. Harlan was too proud and too crazy to ever listen to reason. I hate to say it, because I liked his daddy, but sometimes father and son are just more different than seems possible."

At one time The Kid would have said the same thing about himself and Frank Morgan. But time had opened his eyes and he'd come to realize their true natures weren't that different after all.

"So you're at loose ends again?" Constance asked as they reached the saloon.

"I guess so."

"Then maybe you could take Jared back to his daughter's place in Wichita, once he's healthy enough to travel."

The Kid frowned in surprise. "I sort of had the idea he'd stay here. That maybe you would . . ."

"Take care of him?" Constance finished as The Kid's voice trailed off. "Believe me, I thought about it. It was good to see him again, and that old spark . . ." She cleared her throat and glanced down at the boardwalk for a second. "Maybe some of it is still there. But that doesn't mean I'm suited to take on a responsibility like that. Anyway, it's good to pay a visit to the past now and then, but you can't live there, Kid. All a person really has is today."

He knew that was true. He'd had his own struggles as he tried to come to grips with it.

"Anyway, she's his daughter and I guess she loves him," Constance went on. "I'm sure she's worried half to death about him. If you're not headed any place in particular, well, then, Wichita wouldn't be out of your way, would it?"

"Maybe not," The Kid said. "But it would take a while to get there, and I'd have to ride herd on the marshal every step of the way."

"You can do it. From what I've seen of you, you're a pretty capable young fella."

"I'll give it some thought," but he already knew what his answer was probably going to be. Jared Tate had saved his life twice. He owed the old lawman.

The best way to pay that debt might be to see to it Tate made it back home where he belonged.

122

Chapter 15

The Kid spent the next two weeks in Copperhead Springs while Riley Cumberland got back on his feet. The county sheriff, who was as upset about the whole situation as Constance had predicted, assigned a deputy full-time to the settlement while Cumberland was recuperating, but The Kid wanted to keep an eye on things himself. It wasn't that he didn't trust the sheriff, but the man was obviously skeptical of some of the claims made against Harlan Levesy.

The arrival of a special investigator from the state capital, prompted by a wire to the governor from Claudius Turnbuckle, went a long way toward settling things down. The Browning financial interests held stock in the railroad, a number of banks, and a couple meat packing plants, and The Kid didn't feel the least bit guilty about wielding that influence when it was necessary.

The investigator talked to just about everyone in town. When he was finished, he let the sheriff know his report to the governor would state it was his opinion the citizens of Copperhead Springs had acted in self-defense and had been perfectly justified in taking action against Harlan Levesy. It was hard to argue with that.

The Kid also sent a wire to Tate's daughter Bertha Edwards in Wichita. He wanted to let her know where her father was and that he was alive and well.

The woman's response was a curt, perfunctory thank you, which caused The Kid to frown slightly as he read it. He knew it was almost impossible to tell what someone was feeling from words printed on a telegraph flimsy, but he'd expected a more excited and relieved response from her.

As for the former marshal himself, true to Doc Franklin's prediction, he was up and around in a couple days after suffering that minor wound. He split his time between the Trailblazer and the marshal's office. Constance had given him a room on the saloon's second floor for sleeping, and she or one of her bartenders kept an eye on him all the time he wasn't with The Kid. The arrangement worked out well. Tate didn't have a chance to go wandering off again.

While they were all in the saloon one evening, The Kid broached the idea of taking Tate back to his daughter's home in Wichita.

"Wichita?" Tate repeated with a frown. "Why would I want to go to Wichita?"

"Because that's where you live, Jared," Constance said.

Tate shook his head. "No, I live here in Copperhead Springs," he insisted. "I'm the marshal here."

"We've talked about this before," Constance said with a visible effort to remain patient. "You're not the marshal here anymore. You live in Wichita with your daughter."

"Bertha? Why, she's just a little girl."

Constance sighed. "You've just got to trust me, honey. It'll be better for everybody if you let The Kid here take you home."

Tate got a stubborn look on his face. Most of the time he was friendly and willing to go along with whatever people said, but when he was challenged too much, he dug in his heels and wouldn't budge.

"We'll talk about it later, Marshal." The Kid had seen the look before and knew it wouldn't do any good to continue the discussion. In half an hour, Tate would have no memory of it, and might be in a more receptive mood.

Still in a huff, Tate got up and went over to the bar to talk to one of the bartenders. The Kid and Constance watched him go. She sighed again.

"This is liable to turn into a problem," The Kid said. "I can't very well hogtie him, put him on a horse, and take him back to Wichita against his will."

"I know. Even though that would be the best thing for him." Constance shook her head. "Going home, I mean. Not the hogtying part."

The Kid took a sip of beer from the mug in front of him. "You know, I've been wondering. It's pretty obvious you and the marshal were, well, more than just friends. But I haven't heard any-thing about him being married, and that daughter of his had to come from somewhere. You're not . . . ?"

"Bertha's mama?" Constance stared across the table at him and then snorted. "Good Lord, no."

"Well, then?"

"You're asking me to dredge up a lot of ancient history and gossip about it, Kid. Funny, you didn't strike me as the type."

"Indulge me," The Kid said with a shrug. "Maybe it'll help me figure out a way to talk Jared into going back to Wichita without giving trouble about it."

"All right, all right. But I think you really just want to hear the juicy parts."

The Kid chuckled.

"Jared was married when he came here to Copperhead Springs to take the job as marshal. Brought a wife and a little girl with him. The wife's name was Priscilla, and although I hate to speak ill of the dead, the name suited her. She was a little priss, sure enough."

"So the marshal's a widower?"

"I'll get to that," Constance said. "You're the one who insisted on hearing this story, so just shut up and let me tell it my own way."

The Kid smiled and lifted his beer mug in a signal for her to go on.

"I can't even rightly blame Priscilla for being

the way she was. Jared had dragged her all over the Great Plains, from one little cow town to another, while he was working as a lawman. Almost any woman was going to get tired of living like that."

"You probably wouldn't have," The Kid said, thinking of the way she had wielded that shotgun during the battle.

Constance snorted again. "I said almost any woman. I never claimed to fit in with the rest of the herd. Anyway, almost as soon as they got here, you could tell there was trouble between 'em, but I never heard Jared say a bad word about Priscilla. The same wasn't true the other way around. And the girl . . . well, she was in a bad spot, I guess, and eventually she had to pick a side. She picked her mama."

The Kid nodded slowly. "I guess in a situation like that it's not surprising Jared turned to somebody else for a little comfort."

Constance's eyes suddenly burned with anger as she slapped a hand down on the table so sharply it made the other people in the room look around. She leaned forward and said fiercely, "Don't you ever say that again . . . or even think it. Jared Tate was my friend, yes, but he never laid a hand on me, never said anything the least bit improper, while his wife was still alive. He'd have staked himself to an anthill before he'd do something like that."

"Sorry," The Kid murmured. "I just figured—"

"Well, don't. Jared's an honorable man. Always has been and always will be, no matter . . . no matter what else has been taken away from him."

The other people in the saloon had gone back to their drinking and gambling. The Kid let silence hang between him and Constance for a moment, then said, "I guess something must have happened to Mrs. Tate. Did she get sick?"

"Something happened, all right," Constance said grimly. "Brick Cantrell came to town."

The Kid's eyebrows rose. "Cantrell? The army deserter and outlaw the marshal captured?"

"That's right. You've heard about how Cantrell's bunch raided Copperhead Springs. What I didn't tell you was Priscilla Tate was hit by one of the bullets flying around during the fight."

"So when Jared led the posse after Cantrell, he was avenging his wife, too."

"Yeah, but he didn't know it at the time. He knew she was hurt, but she was still alive when he rode out after Cantrell." Constance sighed. "Some folks thought badly of him for that, I reckon, but for Jared it was just a matter of having a job to do. Besides, he didn't know she wasn't going to pull through. She took a turn for the worse after he left with the posse."

Constance paused and looked down at the table as if gathering her thoughts . . . or her will to go on. "Priscilla was out of her head from the fever a lot of the time. I sat with her quite a bit. Wasn't much anybody could do for her once the poison started spreading through her body except keep her cool and hope she could fight it off. She raved about how it was all Jared's fault. She said some other things, too—"

Again Constance had to stop, and when she went on, she was looking at The Kid solemnly. "I swear, if you ever breathe a word of this to Jared or to anybody else, I'll hunt you down and make you sorry you were ever born, Kid. I mean it. Especially don't tell Jared."

"Not a word," The Kid promised. "Swear to God."

"He won't be able to spare you from my wrath if you go to blabbing." She breathed out another sigh. "Anyway, while Priscilla was out of her head, she said some things that made me wonder if, well, if Jared was really Bertha's daddy. Nothing I could be sure about, mind you. You can never really be sure about the ravings of somebody who's dying like that. But she said enough to make me wonder.

"It didn't really change anything, of course. Jared didn't know. He loved the girl like she was his own, and hell, maybe she is. I was the only one who knew, and I wasn't going to say anything. Priscilla's fever finally broke, there at the last, but it was too late. She was too weak, and she slipped away. By the time Jared got back with Cantrell, she was already buried. Despite all the trouble between them, I think he nearly broke, then. But he still had his duty. He delivered Cantrell to Fort Hays himself."

"He remembers that. I've heard him talking about it. But he never said anything to me about his wife dying about the same time."

"Maybe there are some memories where it's a blessing to have them drift away from you," Constance said. "That's why I don't want you bringing up any of this with Jared. No point in stirring up a lot of old pain."

The Kid sipped his beer and nodded. "You're right about that."

"After all that," Constance continued, "after a year or so had passed . . . well, like I said, Jared and I had always been friendly. That was when he turned to me for a little comfort, as you put it, Kid, but to tell the truth, I reckon he was comforting me as much as I was comforting him. You might not guess it to look at me, but it's never been easy being the big, brassy saloon-keeper. In the minds of a lot of people I'm not much better than a whore. Maybe what I did with Jared just confirmed that, but it never felt that way to me."

"I'm sure it never did to him, either."

Her voice took on a brisk, more businesslike tone. "Jared started sending Bertha back to Wichita during the summers to visit with some of

Priscilla's relatives. During one of those trips, when she was almost grown, she met a boy, and when she went back the next summer he was waiting for her with a ring. They settled down there. He's a clerk in some lawyer's office. Jared stayed on here. He told me he'd decided Copperhead Springs was the last place he was going to wear a lawman's badge." She sighed. "He was right about that. A few more years went by and it started getting obvious he wasn't quite the man he used to be. It was a while before any of us realized how bad it had really gotten. It wasn't until he ran out in the street and started shooting one day, yelling that the Cantrell gang was attacking."

"And there were no outlaws," The Kid guessed.

"Not a one," Constance replied with a shake of her head. "Jared had taken on Riley Cumberland as a deputy, sort of as a favor to Bert since the two of them were friends and Riley was a pretty shiftless kid. Bert was afraid he might go off and become an outlaw if he didn't have something to keep him on the straight and narrow. Once we got Jared calmed down after that little shooting spree—and nobody was hurt, thank God—the town council got together and asked Riley to take over as marshal. Plenty people doubted the kind of job he'd do, but give him credit, he's been a good lawman for us."

"Other than knuckling under to Harlan Levesy."

Constance grimaced. "He was in a bad spot. One man couldn't do anything against all those gunnies." Her eyes narrowed as she looked at The Kid. "Although you sort of did, didn't you?"

"I had a lot of help. The rest of the town deserves more credit than I do."

"Most of them would still be cowering in their beds every time the Broken Spoke hands came around, if not for you," she said bluntly. "They never would have backed Riley's play like that, and he knew it. He tried to keep it the best way he could so the fewest people got hurt."

"That's about all he could do," The Kid agreed. "How'd you talk Jared into going to live with his daughter in Wichita?"

"It wasn't easy, I can tell you that. I wound up having to take him myself. I'd do it again, but I'm too old for a trip like that. Besides, I don't know if I could stand it again. That's why . . ."

"That's why you asked me to do it," The Kid said.

"Yeah. If that makes me a bad person—"

"It doesn't."

Constance placed her hands flat on the table. "Well, that's the story. Good enough gossip for you?"

"More like tragedy in some respects," The Kid said.

"Life usually is." She nodded toward the bar. "Here he comes."

Jared ambled back over to the table carrying a mug of beer. He sat down next to Constance. "What have you two been talking about?"

She smiled at him. "I was just telling The Kid about how I got a letter from Bertha saying she sure would like for you to come for a visit, Jared."

"Bertha," Tate mused. For a second The Kid thought he didn't even remember the name, but then he went on. "It has been a long time since I've seen her and Tim. I really ought to pay them a visit."

"Where is it they live?" The Kid said. "Wichita?"

"That's right."

"Well, if you're going over there, Marshal, I've got a big favor to ask of you."

"Sure, go ahead, Kid."

"You think it would be all right if I rode along with you? I'm headed in that direction myself, and the company would be nice on a long trip like that. Not to mention I'd feel a mite safer having a lawman along."

"I suppose that just makes sense," Tate said. "And I'd admire to have your company, too, Kid. When do you want to go?"

The Kid glanced at Constance. There were still a few hours of daylight left, and he didn't want to waste this opportunity. It might be easier to keep Tate from getting lost in the past if they were away from Copperhead Springs.

When Constance gave him an encouraging nod, he said, "I travel pretty light. I can gather up my gear, pick up a few supplies, and be ready to ride in half an hour."

Tate chuckled. "I like that. No point in burning daylight. I'll be ready, too." He lifted his mug. "To Wichita."

"To Wichita," The Kid replied as he lifted his own mug. That had gone easier than he expected. Of course, they weren't actually on the trail yet.

And even if they managed to get started, he was pretty sure the trip itself wouldn't be easy. He expected challenges every foot of the way.

Chapter 16

Constance hugged them before they mounted up to ride away. Not surprising, the embrace she gave Tate lingered longer than the one The Kid got, which he didn't mind. It was possible Constance would never see her old friend and lover again.

Tears shone in her eyes as she turned back to The Kid, but with her usual hard-boiled attitude, she managed not to shed them.

"Don't you let anything happen to him," she warned. "If you do, I'll never forgive you, and you don't want me holdin' a grudge against you."

"No, I don't think I do," The Kid agreed with a smile. "Don't worry."

"I swear, Constance, you talk like I'm a little kid who needs somebody to look after me," Tate said. "You don't have to be like that. I'm fine. Nothing wrong with me. I'm sharp as a tack, just like I always was."

That was one of the pernicious things about Tate's condition, The Kid thought. At this moment, the old lawman completely believed what he was saying . . . because he couldn't remember all the times when it wasn't true.

"Don't get your feathers ruffled," Constance said. "I was about to tell *you* the same thing about *him*. We owe The Kid a lot. I don't want anything to happen to him."

Tate nodded. "Oh. I understand now. Well, like he told you, don't worry. We'll look after each other."

"Sounds like a good plan," The Kid agreed.

Several of the townsmen gathered to shake hands and say good-bye as well, among them Doc Franklin, Riley Cumberland, and Bert Cumberland. The marshal hadn't fully recovered from his injuries, but he was getting around fairly well.

"The town is in good hands," Tate told Cumberland as he shook with him. "I wouldn't be leaving otherwise."

"I really appreciate that, Marshal. I'll try to live up to it a little better than I have sometimes in the past."

"You'll do fine," Tate assured him.

With their farewells said, The Kid and Tate swung up into their saddles, waved to the people they were leaving behind, and rode out of Copperhead Springs.

"I'm looking forward to seeing my daughter and her family," Tate said as they left the settlement behind them. "But I already know it'll be good to get back home after our visit."

The Kid didn't say anything. There was a good possibility Jared Tate would never set foot in Copperhead Springs again, but he didn't see any reason to point that out. Even if he did, Tate would soon forget it.

They were able to cover only a few miles before the hour grew late enough to start looking for a good campsite. The Kid hadn't expected to travel very far. He'd just wanted to get started while Tate's mind seemed to be fairly clear and the old lawman was being cooperative.

They spread their bedrolls in a small, grassy hollow. There was no water nearby, but their canteens were full so that wasn't a problem. The café in Copperhead Springs had sent food with them, so they didn't even have to worry about preparing a meal, but The Kid brewed a pot of coffee.

"Do we need to take turns standing watch?" Tate asked as he sipped from his cup after supper.

"You think that's necessary?"

"Well, you never know when a Pawnee or Kiowa raiding party might come along."

The Kid figured it had been at least ten years, maybe longer, since any war parties had haunted those parts. Except in isolated places along the Mexican border where Apaches still raided from time to time, as The Kid knew from personal experience, the threat of Indian warfare was over.

He said carefully, "I haven't heard about any trouble from hostiles recently, Marshal. I think we'll be fine."

"There are bands of roving bandits, too," Tate insisted. "Brick Cantrell and his renegades are out there somewhere, and they could strike any time."

"That buckskin horse of mine is a mighty good sentry," The Kid said. "If any other horses come around, he'll let us know. Same with Indians or wild animals."

"Well, in that case I guess we might as well turn in and get a good night's sleep."

"That's what I was thinking." The Kid cleaned up the little bit that needed doing after supper, checked on the horses, and then the two of them rolled up in their blankets. Even though the weather was warm, by morning it would be a little chilly out on the prairie.

The Kid had been telling the truth about counting on the buckskin to warn them if any strange men or horses came around, but he was also relying on his own instincts, which had been honed quite sharp by the dangers of the past few years. He knew he would sleep lightly.

He dozed off easily, a habit frontiersmen developed, and had no idea how long he had been asleep when something roused him. His eyes came open and he was awake instantly, in time to see a dark shape looming over him. He heard the metallic ratcheting of a gun being cocked.

The Kid threw himself to the side, the bedroll impeding him slightly. When the gun roared the bullet came close enough for him to feel its warmth against his cheek as he rolled out of the way barely in time. He threw the blankets off and swept his leg around, catching the calves of the man who'd just tried to kill him.

The man let out a startled yell as The Kid jerked his legs out from under him. The gun blasted again, but was pointed harmlessly at the night sky as the man fell.

As The Kid surged to his feet, he grabbed the Colt from the holster he'd left lying close beside him. He almost fired, but instead stepped forward and swung his leg in a kick, catching the gunman's wrist and knocking the man's weapon flying.

He stepped back and leveled his gun. "Don't move!" He was worried this skulker could have already harmed Marshal Tate.

He didn't have to worry about that, he discovered with a shock as a second later Tate said from the ground, "You'd better go ahead and kill me, Cantrell. If you don't, I'll ventilate your mangy hide as soon as I get the chance!"

The Kid stood with his heart slugging in his chest, trying to wrap his brain around the fact that it was Tate who had just tried to blow his brains out . . . and come mighty close to succeeding!

After a moment, he said, "Marshal, listen to me! I'm not Brick Cantrell. It's me, Kid Morgan. You know me."

"I never heard of any Kid Morgan. I've been on your trail for weeks, Cantrell." Tate sat up and rubbed his wrist where The Kid had kicked him. "You're a deserter and an outlaw, and I'm going to take you in."

The Kid muttered a curse, holstered his Colt, and backed off to the glowing embers of their campfire. Keeping a close eye on Tate, he knelt and stirred the embers back to life, feeding in some buffalo chips to make the flames grow brighter.

"Look at me, Marshal. I don't know what Brick Cantrell looked like, but you can tell I'm not him."

"You could be wearing a disguise," Tate said, but The Kid heard doubt creeping into his voice.

"No. You know better. You know who I am, if you'll just stop and think about it."

The glow from the fire lit up Tate's weathered old face, which was more haggard than usual. He stared across at The Kid, who couldn't tell if he saw any signs of recognition in the old lawman's eyes or not.

Finally Tate said hesitantly, "Kid? Is that you?"

The Kid sighed in relief. "That's right. You remember me now? Kid Morgan? We've known each other for almost three weeks, and we left Copperhead Springs together this afternoon. We're on our way to Wichita so you can visit your daughter and her husband."

"Copperhead Springs . . . I know that name. I . . . I used to live there."

"You were the marshal there for years, but you're retired now. Remember?"

"Of course I remember," Tate snapped, abruptly losing his tentative, confused attitude. "Do you think I'm some sort of idiot?"

"No, sir, not at all."

"There were some men . . . bad men . . . and we fought side by side against them. And . . . and Constance was there . . ."

"That's right."

Tate glared at him. "Did you just *kick* me? What the hell did you do that for?"

"I'm sorry, Marshal," The Kid said. "That was my mistake. Reckon I, uh, was dreaming or something and woke up thinking you were a bad hombre."

"Maybe I'd better move my bedroll a little farther away if you're prone to doing things like that."

"No, it won't happen again." Although to be honest, The Kid wasn't sure how he was going to prevent something similar from occurring. "Why don't you go back to your bedroll and try to get some sleep? We'll be on the trail a long time tomorrow."

Tate got to his feet and gave The Kid a suspicious frown. "Can I trust you? No more crazy shenanigans?"

"I give you my word on it, Marshal."

"All right, then."

Tate hadn't mentioned his gun, and The Kid wasn't about to bring up the subject. He waited until the old lawman had rolled up in the blankets again and didn't move until Tate's deep, regular breathing testified that he was asleep.

The Kid walked quietly to the area where the marshal's gun had landed and searched until he found the weapon lying in the grass. He opened the cylinder and unloaded it, then stowed away the bullets and the gun in his gear.

Tate was bound to think of the gun eventually and want to know where it was, and The Kid had no idea what he would say then. It hadn't occurred to him Tate might be dangerous to himself and to innocent folks around him. He might be fuzzy about what year it was, or whether he was still the marshal, but he'd always known who needed shot and who didn't.

The Kid knew he couldn't risk letting Tate carry a gun anymore.

But he would think about that in the morning.

It was the middle of the night and he just wanted to sleep.

Despite that wish, sleep was quite a while coming.

The next morning, Tate seemed to have no memory of the incident. From time to time he moved his hand around and frowned at his wrist, as if he were trying to remember how he might have hurt himself, but he didn't say anything about it.

The Kid had been awake first, and taken Tate's holster and shell belt and put them away, too, hoping if the marshal didn't see them, he wouldn't think to ask about the gun. Surely he hadn't gone around packing iron when he lived with his daughter. Wichita was a big city. The Kid figured they probably had laws about such things. He decided not to say anything else about Tate being a frontier lawman, not wanting to stir up those memories.

The marshal seemed to be in a good mood, like they were on some sort of outing. The Kid supposed that was true. Tate had gone off on an adventure, and now he was returning home.

They made breakfast of the beef, beans, and biscuits left over from what they'd had the night before, then saddled up and rode out, following the trail leading east. Tate talked about everything under the sun, mostly about people The Kid had never heard of. He didn't mind. It seemed to keep Tate happy.

In the middle of the day they stopped for lunch, then pushed on again. They had seen a few riders in the distance during the day, probably cowboys working on the ranches in the area, but it was a couple hours after noon before they encountered anyone on the trail. The Kid saw something up ahead and realized it was a wagon stopped at the side of the rough road. The vehicle was canted over, appearing to have lost a wheel.

Two men stood beside the wagon looking disconsolately at it, as if they were trying to figure out what to do. The Kid was no expert on such things, but as he and Tate rode up he looked at the wagon and decided the nut had come off the left rear wheel, allowing the wheel to slip off its hub. As long as the nut wasn't lost, or if they had an extra one, the problem wouldn't be too difficult to remedy.

"Howdy," he said as he and Tate reined in. "Can we give you fellas a hand?"

The two men had heard them approaching, but didn't turn to look at them until they stopped. One of them was big and shaggy like a bear, wearing a duster and a battered old top hat. He carried two revolvers tucked behind a sash wrapped around his ample middle. The other man was smaller, reminding The Kid of a weasel with his sharp face and mean eyes. He was hatless, with leather trousers and a wool shirt. What looked like an old cap-and-ball pistol rode in a holster at his waist.

The Kid didn't like the looks of either man. When he glanced at the mules hitched to the wagon, he saw scars of old wounds on their backs where they had been whipped repeatedly. He knew mules could be balky and frustrating, but the sort of cruelty represented by those marks rubbed him the wrong way.

"Lost a wheel," the big man said unnecessarily. "I guess if you want to help me lift the wagon, my partner can slip it back on."

"All right."

As The Kid dismounted, he glanced at the back of the wagon. It was loaded with bulky cargo covered by canvas and tied down. What they were hauling was none of his business, of course, but the furtive looks the smaller man kept shooting back and forth between him and the wagon made him a little leery of trouble.

The Kid hoped he hadn't made a mistake by deciding to be a Good Samaritan. He wanted to get the wheel back on the wagon as quickly as possible so the two men could be on their way and he and the marshal could be on theirs.

He and the big man stepped to the drooping corner of the vehicle. The Kid was on the side of the wagon, the other man around at the rear. As they bent to get a good hold, the big man said in a friendly fashion, "Where you fellas headed?"

"Wichita," The Kid answered, not offering any more information than that. He wanted to get this chore finished and be on their way again.

When they were set, The Kid shouted "All right . . . heave!"

With grunts of effort, they lifted the wagon. Through clenched teeth, the big man said, "All right . . . Selmon . . . get the wheel . . . back on there."

"I don't think so." The man called Selmon stepped back quickly, pulled his old percussion pistol from its holster, and swung the barrel back and forth between The Kid and Tate. "That old man's the marshal from Copperhead Springs! Don't you recognize him, Benny? They're on to us, and we're gonna have to kill 'em both!"

Chapter 17

"What are you doing?" Tate exclaimed. "Put that gun down, you fool."

The big man, Benny, let out a startled curse. "Selmon, you shouldn't oughta—"

It was too late for that. Selmon had drawn his gun, and The Kid could tell he was ready to shoot. The man's piggish little eyes gleamed with the desire to kill.

The Kid let go of the wagon and jerked his

body backward as the old pistol erupted with a dull boom. Flame stabbed from the muzzle, followed by a gout of black smoke.

The balls fired by those old percussion weapons didn't travel nearly as fast as slugs from modern cartridges. The Kid heard one drone past his ear, sounding remarkably like a hummingbird.

Benny screeched in pain, and The Kid thought Selmon's shot had struck him. Then a glance told him the wagon's weight had been too much for Benny to hold up by himself. He'd lost his grip, and the rear corner of the wagon had fallen on his foot.

With Benny no threat for the moment, The Kid concentrated on Selmon. The man tried to swing the pistol in line again, but he was too slow by far. The Kid could have drawn twice before Selmon could get off another shot.

As it was, the Colt flashed from his holster and his finger was on the trigger, ready to fire, when Marshal Tate launched himself out of the saddle and tackled Selmon from behind. The Kid stopped himself from squeezing the trigger so he wouldn't take a chance on hitting the old lawman.

Tate and Selmon crashed to the ground. Selmon had managed to cock the pistol again, and the jolt made it go off. The ball plowed into the trail, leaving a furrow in the dirt.

Selmon twisted around and threw an elbow into Tate's chest, knocking the lawman loose from him. Like a snake, he writhed to the side and started to swing the percussion pistol at Tate's head like a club.

Before the heavy weapon landed, The Kid's boot came down on Selmon's wrist, pinning it to the ground. Selmon yelped as The Kid's weight bore down on his bones and flesh. His fingers opened, releasing the gun.

The Kid reached down with his left hand and plucked the gun from Selmon's hand. He pointed the Colt still in his right hand at Selmon's face. "You'd better stop fussing. I'm in no mood for this."

"You . . . you . . ."

The Kid bore down with his boot heel on Selmon's wrist.

"Ahhhhh!"

"What did I tell you about that? Now, I'm going to step back, and you're going to sit up and stay right there. Because if you don't, I'll shoot you. Don't doubt that for a second."

Selmon opened his mouth, but if he was about to curse at The Kid, he thought better of it. His mouth snapped shut and stayed that way as he sat up.

The Kid stepped back, keeping Selmon covered as he asked, "Marshal, are you all right?"

Tate climbed slowly to his feet and brushed the dust off his clothes. "I'm fine. You think these two have learned their lesson, Kid?"

The Kid looked at Selmon cradling his painful wrist with his other hand, then at Benny, who was slumped against the wagon whimpering, trapped by the vehicle's weight on his foot.

"I don't know," The Kid said in answer to Tate's question. "Let's see what they were so worried about." He tucked Selmon's revolver behind his gun belt and moved closer to the wagon. Reaching into the back to grasp the canvas cover, he threw aside one corner and revealed several wooden crates packed with bottles and jugs full of clear liquid.

He had a pretty good idea what it was. "A load of moonshine." He frowned at Selmon. "That's what this was all about? You were willing to shoot us over some damned white lightning?"

"It's illegal," Selmon said with a whine in his voice, "and that old fella's a lawman. I remember seein' him in Copperhead Springs wearin' a badge. For all I know, you're one of those damned star packers, too, mister."

"Well, you're behind the times, as well as mistaken. Marshal Tate's retired, and even if he wasn't, as long as you stayed out of Copperhead Springs with that stuff he wouldn't have any reason to arrest you. And I'm not a lawman at all . . . just a man who gets mighty upset when somebody shoots a gun at him."

"You ain't hurt," Selmon said. "Benny and me, we're the ones in pain."

"Benny more than you, I'd say, since that wagon full of hooch fell on his foot."

Benny chose that moment to throw back his head and bellow like a wounded bull. "Oh, Gaaawwd, it hurts!"

"See?" The Kid said. "What do you think we ought to do about that?"

"We, uh, oughta get it off of him, I reckon."

"How are we going to do that? You and I might be able to lift the wagon enough for him to pull his foot out, but I'd have to holster my gun, and after the stunt you just pulled, I'm not sure I want to do that."

"I'm not armed. I can't do anything else," Selmon said. "I swear. Help me get that thing offa him, mister. Please."

The Kid thought about it. He was still angry about Selmon trying to shoot him. And after seeing the way they'd mistreated their mules he wasn't feeling very sympathetic toward either man. But he didn't enjoy seeing Benny suffer. Just because *they* were cruel didn't mean he had to be.

He told Selmon, "You stand where I can see you. Marshal, keep an eye on him, too, and sing out if he looks like he's going to try anything funny."

"I sure will," Tate said.

The Kid pouched his iron and moved around Benny. One at a time, he pulled the guns from behind the sash around the big man's waist, tossing them well out of reach. He got a grip on the wagon bed and said, "On three . . . one . . . two . . . three!"

He and Selmon heaved on the wagon, lifting it enough for Benny to grab hold of his leg and drag his foot out from under it.

As soon as Benny was clear, The Kid let the wagon down again and stepped back, resting his hand on the butt of his Colt.

Benny sat down hard, unable to stand up. Selmon scrambled over to him. "Let's get that boot offa there so we can see how bad you're hurt." He glanced up at The Kid. "That's all right, ain't it?"

The Kid nodded. "Go ahead."

Benny screamed as Selmon worked the boot off. The sock was soaked with blood. Selmon peeled that off as well, also accompanied by screams, and revealed an ugly gash in Benny's foot.

It wasn't mangled as much as The Kid had expected. Since the other wheels were still on the wagon, not all of its weight had come down on Benny's foot.

"I'm plumb ruined," Benny sobbed. "I'll never be able to walk again."

"I think you will," The Kid said, "but not if you keep going around trying to kill people. You won't have to worry about your foot because you'll get yourself shot."

"Are you gonna turn us over to the law?" Selmon asked as he used the tail of his shirt to wipe away some of the blood on Benny's foot.

"It's not my responsibility to put moonshiners out of business. As for taking a shot at me . . . well, maybe by the time I'm through with you, you'll have been punished enough without bringing the law into this."

Selmon gave him a worried look. "What else are you gonna do? You already pert near busted my wrist, and Benny's foot's all messed up."

"That's Benny's fault for letting go of the wagon. As for what else I'm going to do, those mules are coming with us."

"You can't do that!" Selmon protested immediately. "Them mules are ours. That'd be stealin'!"

"It's not as bad as trying to shoot somebody," The Kid pointed out. "I don't like the way you've treated them."

Benny glared at Selmon. "I told you not to whip those jugheads so dang much!"

"Shut up! You're a jughead your own self!" Selmon looked at The Kid. "You're gonna leave us here with no team and a wheel off the wagon?"

"That's right."

"What'll we do with all that 'shine'?"

"I'd get a bottle and use some of it to clean that wound on Benny's foot. Then you can sit around and drink the rest of it for all I care."

"This ain't right. It ain't fair—"

"Save your breath," The Kid interrupted. "And be grateful. I thought about burning it."

Selmon looked like he wanted to say something else, but kept his mouth shut.

The Kid told Tate, "Keep watching them," and went to the front of the wagon to unhitch the mules. He tied their harnesses together so they would be easier to lead.

Selmon took The Kid's suggestion and poured whiskey from one of the bottles over the gash in Benny's foot, causing Benny to howl at the bite of the fiery liquor on raw flesh. The Kid saw him wiggling his toes and figured no bones were broken. Benny was lucky his foot hadn't been crushed.

"All right, Marshal, I guess we're ready to go," The Kid said. "I'll lead these mules if you can lead our pack horses."

"Sure, I can do that," Tate said. They got mounted up and paused beside the spot where Selmon and Benny were sitting on the ground behind the wagon.

The Kid fixed Selmon with a hard stare. "Anybody takes a shot at me, I generally go ahead and kill him right then and there. I've made an exception in your case, but if I ever see you again, and your hand is anywhere near a gun when I do, I won't wait to see what you're planning to do with it. I'll just go ahead and shoot you. You remember that."

"I'll remember," Selmon said in a surly growl. It sounded as much like a threat as a promise.

"I know what you're thinking. You'll let this fester and gnaw at you and tell yourself that one of these days you'll get even with me. But you won't. You'll just get dead." The Kid hoped his little speech would be enough to get through the fog of hatred in Selmon's brain, but he didn't believe it would be. Sooner or later he'd probably have to kill the weaselly little varmint . . . unless, of course, their trails never crossed again, which was certainly possible.

As he and Tate rode away, leaving the wagon and the two moonshiners behind, The Kid said, "Thanks for helping out back there, Marshal, but you'd better let me handle the gunplay, if there is any from here on out."

"I reckon I'll have to," Tate said. "I seem to have misplaced my Colt. Can't find it anywhere."

"I'm sorry about that," The Kid replied, knowing good and well the marshal's gun, gun belt, and ammunition were tucked away in his gear.

"That's all right. I'm getting a mite forgetful, the older I get, I suppose. I'll buy another gun when we get to Wichita."

The Kid didn't say anything. It would be up to the marshal's daughter to keep him from getting his hands on another gun.

Late that afternoon they came to a small farm.

The Kid could tell by looking at the place it wasn't doing that well. The house needed work, and so did the barn.

But the rawboned man who walked out to greet them had a friendly smile on his face, and he was trailed by a couple kids, a boy and a girl, who seemed just as friendly, as did the big shaggy dog that bounded out to bark at them.

"You fellas looking for a place to spend the night?" the farmer asked. "Plenty of room in the loft, and my wife'll be glad to put another couple plates on the table."

The Kid thumbed back his hat. "We're obliged for the offer, friend, but what we're really looking for is a place to leave these mules for a while. We're sort of in a hurry, and they're slowing us down."

The farmer walked over to the mules and studied them, shooting a glance at The Kid as he did so. "They're good-looking animals, but someone's treated them pretty badly."

"That's what I thought, so my friend and I took them off the hands of the men who did that. Made a trade with them."

That was true, The Kid thought. He and Tate took the mules, and he didn't shoot Selmon and Benny. That was a fair trade as far as he was concerned.

The farmer said, "I might've been tempted to do more than just trade if I ran into somebody who treats animals like this. You familiar with the story of Balaam and the ass in the Bible?"

"I remember hearing about it," The Kid said. "You think it would be all right for us to leave these mules here for a while? I'd give you some money to pay for their feed and all."

The little boy said, "Pa, you know we sure could use a good team of mules—"

"These men aren't offering to give us the mules, Tom."

"No, but we wouldn't mind if you were to work 'em some," The Kid said. "Work's good for mules."

"And boys," the farmer said with a glance at his son.

"Anyway," The Kid went on, "as long as you take good care of them, you're welcome to use them for whatever chores they might be good for. We'll come back for them one of these days, but it might be a while."

The Kid could tell by the look in the farmer's eyes the man understood and was grateful for it. No man liked to accept obvious charity in front of his children. Of course, to The Kid's way of thinking it wasn't exactly charity, since he and Tate had to do something with the animals. He sure didn't want to have to lead a bunch of mules all the way to Wichita.

"You got a deal," the farmer said as he held up a hand. The Kid reached down and clasped it firmly.

"And the invitation to supper still stands."

"We're obliged, but we need to be moving on. Got more ground to cover before nightfall." The Kid reached into his pocket, took out a couple double eagles, and passed them unobtrusively to the farmer. "To help out with their feed bill."

The man nodded and swallowed hard, evidently not trusting himself to speak.

A few minutes later, with the youngsters waving good-bye and the dog barking behind them, The Kid and Tate rode on without the mules.

The old lawman said quietly, "That was a good thing you did. That sodbuster looked like he could use all the help he can get. Making a hardscrabble farm like that pay off is mighty tough."

"Yeah, but he seemed like the sort who'll make it," The Kid said. "Man's got a place of his own, a nice wife, some kids . . . well, he's got a good start on everything he needs in life, doesn't he?"

"I'd say so," Tate agreed. "You have any of those things, Kid?"

The Kid smiled faintly, trying not to think about the past, as he shook his head. "Nary a one."

Chapter 18

"Gonna kill that son of a bitch," Selmon muttered as he wrapped a makeshift bandage around Benny's injured foot. He had cleaned up the wound as best he could. "Gonna find him and kill him. Try standin' on that."

Benny used the wagon to help him stand up and winced as he rested a little weight on the bad foot. When he rested a little more on it, he yelled and clutched harder at the wagon, lifting the foot again.

"I can't stand on it," he said, panting from the pain. "I think . . . I think it's broken."

"Well, you're just gonna have to put up with it," Selmon said. "There ain't nothin' else I can do for you."

"Maybe you could make me a crutch?" Benny suggested.

"Out of what? And we're ten miles or more from anywhere. Even with a crutch, how you gonna walk that far? You can't." Selmon sighed. "I got to leave you here, Benny, while I go for help."

"You . . . you ain't gonna leave me for good, are you?"

"No, of course not, just for a while. Anyway, we can't both go off and leave this here load of moonshine unprotected. Hell, we got all our money tied up in it. You got to stay here and watch over it. That damn varmint tossed your guns out in the grass. I'll go find 'em."

"Can you help me sit down first?"

Selmon rolled his eyes, but he took hold of Benny's arm and supported him. "All right, take it nice and easy."

Benny sat down on the ground next to the wagon, out of the trail. Selmon found his friend's two revolvers and brought them back. He handed one of them to Benny. "I'm keepin' one of these guns since that polecat rode off with mine."

Benny nodded. "That's fine. I don't mind sharin' my shootin' irons."

"I wasn't askin'," Selmon snapped. "Now, I'm countin' on you, Benny. You can't let nothin' happen to this hooch."

"I'll take care of it," Benny promised. "Selmon . . . you ain't really goin' after that fella, are you? He pretty much said he'd shoot you on sight if he ever saw you again."

"After what happened to you, don't you want the score settled with him?"

"Well, sure I would, but I don't know that it's worth gettin' killed over. Anyway, we don't even know who he is. He never said his name."

"We know he's travelin' with that old Marshal Tate from Copperhead Springs. Lotsa folks in these parts know Tate, or at least know of him. He was a reg'lar town tamer for a good long while."

"Reckon he's still pretty tough, judgin' from the way he tackled you."

"He took me by surprise, is all, damn it," Selmon said defensively.

Benny looked down. He and Selmon had been working together long enough for him to know it wasn't wise to push the smaller man too far. Selmon had a loco streak in him and didn't always bother to hold it in.

"Anyway, I'll settle up with those fellas later," Selmon went on. "Right now, I got to do somethin' about this mess we're in. I'll walk to Rutherford's place and get some help there."

"That'll take you half the night," Benny protested.

"You got any better ideas?"

Benny sighed and shook his head. "No, I reckon I don't," he admitted. "You know me, Selmon. I ain't much of one for ideas."

Selmon grunted. "I know. I'm used to doin' the thinkin' for both of us. You just stay here. I'll be back."

"I ain't goin' nowhere," Benny said dispiritedly. "Not with this busted foot."

Selmon checked the gun he'd kept to make sure dirt hadn't fouled the barrel and found that it appeared to be all right, still in good working condition. With a nod to Benny, he started trudging westward along the trail.

A couple miles from there, a smaller trail turned

off to the north. He and Benny had traveled the route before. That northbound trail ran into an isolated area and after ten miles or so he would come to Rutherford's Store. Despite its name, it was actually a saloon and whorehouse that catered to men on the dodge. Abner Rutherford was a regular customer of the moonshine Selmon and Benny cooked up. He would be willing to help. He wouldn't let a whole wagonload of the stuff go to waste.

It was a long walk. Selmon knew it wouldn't take him half the night, the way Benny had said, but it probably would be well after dark by the time he reached Rutherford's. He hoped nobody would come along in the meantime, kill Benny, and steal the moonshine. He could always get another partner, but he'd hate to lose that hooch.

Cowboys hated to walk. To a cowboy's way of thinking, any chore that couldn't be done from horseback was a chore not worth doing.

Selmon, on the other hand, had never been a cowboy. The work struck him as being way too hard for the amount of money a fella could earn.

Even so, he didn't care much for walking, either, and he liked it less by the time Rutherford's Store came into view. Blisters had sprung up on his feet, and every step sent pain jabbing into them.

He'd hoped somebody would come along with a buggy or a wagon and give him a ride. Even somebody on horseback who'd let him ride double would have been welcome. But Selmon seemed to be the only one who was headed for Rutherford's place.

When he spotted the lights up ahead he felt the impulse to run. The sooner he got there, the sooner he could get off his feet.

He couldn't stand the extra punishment running caused, so he kept moving at the same slow, steady pace, gradually drawing closer to the store. The moon had risen, and along with the stars it provided enough light for him to see the low, rambling sod structure and a number of horses in the corral off to the side. Selmon hoped he could take some of those horses back to the wagon, as well as somebody who'd help him fix the busted wheel.

He stepped through the open doorway into the large, smoky barroom. In a slight nod to the name of the place, a few shelves of supplies and other goods occupied the right end of the room, but nearly all the space was given over to tables and a long, plank bar supported by barrels of whiskey and beer. The left end of the room sported a row of curtained-off cubicles where three or four soiled doves plied their trade.

At the moment, only a couple tables had customers seated at them. A desultory poker game was going on at one of them, while at the other several men were drinking in morose silence.

Nearly a dozen men were crowded up to the bar, where Rutherford and his fat Indian wife served them.

Rutherford spotted Selmon, and his bushy eyebrows lifted in surprise. "I was expectin' you earlier today, Selmon." He waved over the newcomer. "What happened?"

Selmon limped up to the bar, grimacing with every step as he had been for the past five miles. "Benny and me ran into some trouble. Our wagon lost a wheel, then some fellas came along, tried to kill us, and stole our mules."

"Good Lord," Rutherford muttered. "You look like you could use a drink."

"Yeah, and a place to sit. I walked the whole way up here, a good twelve miles." *More like a* bad *twelve miles,* he thought.

"Sit down there at that table. I'll bring you a glass."

"Much obliged," Selmon said with a nod.

It was a great relief to get the weight off his feet. He looked down at his boots and frowned. He was almost afraid to look at the damage done to his feet. Besides, if he took the boots off, hemight not be able to get them back on. The smartest thing was to leave them alone until he rescued Benny and got the wagon to the saloon.

Rutherford came over with a glass and a bottle. The whiskey wasn't as good as the shine Selmon and Benny brewed, but Selmon was happy to get it. He took the glass and gulped it down. A welcome warmth spread through him.

"Tell me what happened," Rutherford urged.

"We were headed up here to make that delivery to you when we lost a nut off one of the back wheels," Selmon explained. He picked up the bottle and splashed more whiskey into the glass. "Damn wheel came all the way off before we realized what was goin' on."

"Shoot, Benny's big enough he should've been able to pick up the wagon so you could put the wheel back on."

Selmon grunted in disgust. "Yeah, you'd think so, wouldn't you? But he couldn't raise it high enough by himself, and if I helped him, there wasn't anybody to slip the wheel back on. Then a couple of fellas came ridin' along."

"The ones who stole your mules."

"That's right. But before they did that . . ." Selmon hesitated as he debated how much to tell Rutherford. He decided not to lie about it. Rutherford was as big a crook as anybody in those parts and had no love for the law.

"We sort of had a run-in with those fellas. One of 'em was that old gunfightin' marshal from over at Copperhead Springs."

Rutherford frowned in confusion. "What are you talkin' about? Riley Cumberland's the marshal at Copperhead Springs. At least he was the last time I heard."

"No, no," Selmon muttered. "I mean old Marshal Tate."

"Jared Tate? Why, he hasn't been a lawman for four or five years, maybe longer."

"Well, I didn't know that, all right?" Selmon tossed off the second drink and wiped the back of his hand across his mouth. "I got better things to do with my time than keep up with who's wearin' a badge and who ain't."

Rutherford looked like he was trying not to smile as he said, "Lemme get this straight. You started a fight with that old retired marshal because you were afraid he was gonna arrest you for haulin' moonshine?"

"It wasn't just him," Selmon said miserably. "He had some young hotshot with him. Could've been a federal man for all I know."

Rutherford couldn't hold in a chuckle. "So you got roughed up by a retired star packer and a kid, and then they stole your mules. You are quite the desperado, Selmon, you really are."

It was all Selmon could do to keep from losing his temper. Through clenched teeth, he said, "I'll settle that score with 'em one of these days. You can bet on that, Ab."

"Yeah, well, what're you gonna do now?"

"I thought maybe you'd let me borrow some horses so I can go back down there and fetch Benny and the wagon."

"Is Benny all right?"

"Yeah, the wagon, uh, sort of fell on his foot and—"

Rutherford laughed again, then shook his head and waved a hand. "I'm sorry. Go on."

"I need a team, and I need somebody to help me get that wheel back on the wagon. Then we can finish deliverin' that load of shine to you."

"If I've got to loan you some horses and lend you a hand, I'll expect a nice discount on the price."

Selmon winced, and it had nothing to do with the pain in his feet. "We're already givin' you the rock-bottom price, Ab—"

"If you're not ready to deal, you can find some help somewhere else."

There wasn't anywhere else, and Rutherford damn well knew it, Selmon thought. He sighed. "All right, we'll knock some off the price."

"A third?"

"A third!" Selmon yelped. "We won't make no money at all, at that price! I was thinkin' . . . five percent?"

"Twenty-five."

They haggled back and forth for a few minutes, and Selmon actually forgot about how much his feet hurt as he got caught up in the negotiating. They settled on twenty percent. Rutherford wouldn't budge from that price.

"We'll head down there to get Benny and the wagon first thing in the mornin'," the proprietor said.

"We can't go tonight?"

Rutherford let out a snort. "Hell, no. The night's half gone, and I plan on sleepin' in my own bed. Tomorrow mornin's soon enough."

Selmon nodded in agreement. There was nothing else he could do.

A shadow fell over the table, causing him to look up. A shaggy-haired man in a buckskin jacket and high-crowned felt hat stood there. The man had a soup-strainer mustache hanging over his mouth, under a prominent beak of a nose. Selmon didn't recognize him.

"Somethin' I can do for you, mister?" he asked, trying not to whine.

"Did I hear you mention Marshal Jared Tate a few minutes ago?" the man asked in a deep, gravelly voice.

"What if I did?" Selmon tried to move his hand closer to the butt of the pistol tucked in his waistband without being obvious about it. "Is he a friend of yours?"

"A friend of mine?" the shaggy stranger repeated. He laughed. "Not hardly. I didn't know he was anywhere around these parts."

"Well, he is, and he ain't a lawman no more. Ain't much better than an owlhoot, if you ask me, the way him and that other fella jumped me and my pard and hurt us and stole our mules."

The stranger shook his head. "That don't sound like Tate. He was always so upright. Acted like he had a ramrod instead of a spine." The man's voice hardened. "And he hid behind that badge of his when he killed my brother. I been waitin' years to get even with him for that."

"I don't know nothin' about that," Selmon said. "All I know is he sure mistreated us."

"How about where he was bound for?" The man leaned over the table and his voice dropped to a low, menacing snarl. "You know that?"

"Take it easy, Carl," Rutherford advised nervously. He glanced at Selmon. "You better answer the question."

"Wichita," Selmon said. For a moment he hadn't been able to remember if either Tate or the other man had said anything about where they were going, but then it had come to him. "The young fella said they were headed for Wichita."

The stranger called Carl straightened. "Wichita's a pretty good ride from here," he mused. "It'll take 'em some time to get there."

"What're you thinkin' about doin'?" Rutherford asked.

"Nothin' you want to know about." Carl tossed a coin on the table. "That'll pay what I owe you. I'm ridin' out."

"Suit yourself."

"Oh, I intend to." An ugly grin stretched Carl's mouth under that soup-strainer. "As soon as I round up my other brothers, we'll suit ourselves just fine."

Selmon figured he wouldn't have to worry about getting his revenge on Tate and the other man. He had a hunch by telling Carl where they could be found, he had just done that.

Chapter 19

The Kid and Marshal Tate reached Dodge City the next day. Since the vast buffalo herds that once covered the prairie for seemingly endless miles were all gone and the railroads had extended their reach into Texas, ending the cattle drive era, Dodge had lost its two main reasons for being. Its boom days were long over, but the settlement clung to existence as a small town serving the needs of the farms and ranches in the surrounding area.

Travelers sometimes stopped there, and The Kid and Tate fell into that category. As they rode into town late in the afternoon, the old lawman said, "I hate to admit it, Kid, but I'm not as young as I used to be. Sleeping out on the trail is hard on these old bones of mine. You reckon we could get rooms in the hotel and spend the night here? Sleep in a real bed?"

"I don't see why not," The Kid answered. "We're not in any big hurry to get where we're going. We can pick up a few more supplies while we're here, too."

They turned their horses toward the Dodge House. The hotel had its own stable out back, so they didn't have to hunt up a livery. After they'd rented adjoining rooms, The Kid turned the horses over to the hostler and carried their gear upstairs.

He found Tate standing at the window in one of the rooms, looking out at the street. He glanced over his shoulder at The Kid. "Lots of memories in this town. The Mastersons, the Earps . . . It was a wild place in the old days, you know, but at the same time so vital, so alive . . . You never knew what was going to happen in Dodge. Now it just seems . . . sleepy." He sighed. "Sort of like me, I guess."

Tate seemed pretty lucid at the moment.

The Kid said, "It'll be getting dark soon. Why don't we go hunt up some supper?"

Tate brightened. "We can go to Delmonico's," he suggested. "Best steaks you'll find this side of Kansas City."

The Kid didn't know if Delmonico's was still there or if it existed only in Tate's memory, but he said, "Sure, Marshal, let's go."

As it turned out, Delmonico's was not only still there, but the food was excellent. Steak, potatoes, greens, corn on the cob, huge fluffy rolls with steam rising from them when torn open, peach cobbler, all washed down with fine coffee . . . Tate had been right. For a sleepy little former cow town, the meal was a lot better than The Kid expected.

When they finished, Tate said, "I'd like to stroll around town a little, Kid, if you don't mind."

"Sure, that's fine," The Kid replied with a shrug. "You can go back to the hotel if you want. I'll be fine."

Tate had seemed fine the whole day. He hadn't done anything odd or displayed any lapses of memory or judgment. The Kid knew he couldn't rely on that condition continuing, though. To keep from offending Tate, he said, "Why don't you show me around? I'd really like to hear about the old days when you were a peace officer here and Dodge City was the Queen of the Prairie."

Tate chuckled. "You shouldn't ask an old man to reminisce. You might get more than you bargained for."

"I'll take my chances," The Kid said with a smile.

"All right, then. Over here is where the Long Branch Saloon used to be . . ."

They spent a pleasant hour walking around town while Tate pointed out the landmarks, the ones still standing as well as the locations of those that were gone, and told at least one story to go with every place they came to. The Kid had heard plenty of yarns from his father over the years, and Tate's were similar, full of colorful characters and blood-and-thunder adventure.

Those must have been exciting times in which

to live, The Kid mused. The West had settled down considerably since then.

Of course, his own life was ample proof there were still pockets of violence on the frontier. With a new century coming soon, people talked about how the Wild West was dead. The Kid knew good and well that wasn't true.

They were ambling back toward the hotel when several men rode into town and dismounted in front of one of the saloons a few doors down from the Dodge House. The Kid didn't pay much attention to them as he and Tate stepped up onto the hotel porch. The glow from the lamps in the lobby came through the windows and lit up their faces.

A man suddenly yelled, "There he is, by God! There's Tate!"

Hearing the menacing tone in that shout, The Kid whirled toward the men who had stopped in front of the saloon. All three of them were clawing at the guns on their hips.

Tate was unarmed and had been ever since he'd mistaken The Kid for Brick Cantrell and tried to shoot him. The Kid grabbed the old lawman's arm with his left hand and gave Tate a hard shove that sent him crashing against the double front doors of the hotel. The doors flew open, and Tate stumbled and fell across the threshold. He was out of the line of fire, at least for the moment.

At the same instant, The Kid's right hand dipped and came up with the Colt. The revolver rose with blinding speed. The three men had cleared leather; they were pretty fast themselves. Shots crashed from their guns.

The Kid heard the wind-rip of a slug past his ear as he triggered twice. One of the would-be assassins went down, doubling over as The Kid's lead punched into his guts.

Standing tall, The Kid thrust his arm out and fired again. A second gunman fell, spinning off his feet from the impact of the bullet.

The tail of The Kid's coat jerked as a shot tugged on it. Almost faster than an eye could blink, he squeezed off two more shots. The last of the gunmen staggered, but didn't go down. He struggled to lift his weapon and get off another shot.

The Kid's revolver was empty. As a precaution he kept the hammer riding on an empty chamber. Only five rounds had been in the gun. Without taking his eyes off the wounded man, he opened the cylinder, dumped the empties, and pulled fresh cartridges from the loops on his gun belt. He thumbed them in, his fingers moving with smooth, practiced efficiency. He snapped the cylinder closed and raised the gun, ready to fire again.

It wasn't necessary. The last man's gun slipped from nerveless fingers and thudded to the boardwalk. The man fell face-first right after it.

But there were only two men in the street, The Kid saw with something of a shock. He had hit all three of the would-be killers, but one of them was gone.

The missing man was the second one who had fallen. The hombre could have crawled off while The Kid was trading shots with the third gunman. The dark mouth of an alley was only a few feet from where he had fallen.

The Kid pressed himself against the wall. For all he knew, the missing man was on his feet and drawing a bead on him from the alley.

"Kid!" Tate called softly from the open doors of the hotel. "Kid, are you all right?"

"I'm fine. Stay back, Marshal. One of the varmints is unaccounted for."

"Who in the world are they?"

"Don't know," The Kid replied curtly. "Somebody with a grudge against you, from the sound of it." He hadn't forgotten how one of the men had yelled out Tate's name just before the shooting started.

A glance at the downed men told him they hadn't moved since they'd fallen. The Kid would have felt better about it if he was sure they were dead, but if he stepped out there to check on them, he'd be making himself a better target.

He watched them from the corner of his eye as he slid along the wall toward the alley. If either of them moved, he'd put another bullet in them.

The street had cleared in a hurry when the shooting started. Enough people in Dodge still remembered the old days and knew to hunt cover when the bullets began to fly.

Shouts of alarm were going up, and The Kid knew it wouldn't be long before the local law arrived on the scene. He needed to find the third man and deal with him before things got more complicated.

As he reached the corner and was about to turn quickly around it and cover the alley with his gun, someone in the hotel yelled, "Look out!"

The roar of a shot immediately followed the warning cry.

The Kid bit back a curse as he whirled away from the alley and lunged toward the hotel entrance. He knew without being told what had happened: the wounded man had made it to a back door and entered the hotel. It was likely he was gunning for Jared Tate.

The Kid leaped through the doors as another shot blasted. Padding flew from an overstuffed chair to his right as a bullet ripped into it.

Tate crouched low behind the chair. He looked to be unharmed so far, but that wasn't likely to last.

The Kid snapped a shot at the gunman crouched behind the front desk counter. Splinters flew as the bullet struck the desk.

The gunman stood, switched his aim, and threw a slug at The Kid. It whistled past his ear.

The Kid fired again. The bullet found its mark,

smashing into the gunman's shoulder and slewing him around sideways. The man threw his gun up for another shot. His weapon and The Kid's Colt blasted at the same time. The man flew backward into the rack holding room keys as The Kid's bullet hammered into his chest.

He bounced off the wall and sprawled across the counter as the gun slid from his fingers and fell to the floor.

As the deafening echoes of the shots began to fade in the lobby, The Kid looked over at Tate. "Are you all right, Marshal?"

Tate nodded. "He nearly winged me, but close doesn't count."

That was certainly true, The Kid thought as he walked quickly across the lobby, keeping the fallen gunman covered as he approached the front desk. He went around the corner of it, grasped the man's shoulder, and shoved him onto the floor. The boneless way he fell told The Kid he was dead.

There was no sign of the clerk. He had lit a shuck out of there just as soon as the trouble started.

"Better stay down," The Kid told Tate as he turned back toward the entrance. "I need to make sure the others aren't a threat anymore."

As he stepped onto the porch, running footsteps came to a stop close by and a man called, "Hold it right there, mister!"

A couple men wearing badges were carrying

shotguns. The Kid held up both hands, the Colt still in his right, to show that he meant no harm.

"Put that gun down and back away from it," one of the lawman ordered.

"I'd be glad to, but one of you had better keep an eye on those two." The Kid nodded to the gunmen in the street. "They're the ones who started this fandango."

"Just do what I told you," the star packer snapped.

The Kid bent and placed his Colt on the porch. He stepped back from it, still keeping his hands in plain sight. He didn't want to give anybody carrying a shotgun an excuse to get nervous and trigger-happy.

The man who'd been doing the talking told his companion, "Check on those two, like he said."

The lawman circled the bodies warily, then came close enough to get a good look at them. "They both look dead to me, Marshal."

"Keep an eye on them," the marshal ordered. To The Kid, he said, "Who are you, mister, and what the hell was all this shooting about?"

"Those two and another one who's inside the hotel tried to ambush me and a friend of mine. They opened fire first."

"The one in the hotel, I reckon he's dead, too?"

The Kid shrugged. "There wasn't time to get fancy."

"You didn't tell me your name."

"It's Morgan—"

"And he's with me," Tate said from the hotel entrance. "I'm Marshal Jared Tate from Copperhead Springs."

That brought a frown to the face of the law badge-toter.

"You're a lawman?"

"Retired," Tate said. "Mr. Morgan and I are on our way to Wichita. What he told you is true, Marshal. Those men attacked us, and he acted in self-defense."

The local man lowered his shotgun slightly. "Why were they gunning for you? Do you know them?"

"Let me take a look, and I might be able to answer that."

The marshal hesitated for a second, then nodded. "Sure, go ahead."

Tate walked along the porch, then stepped down to the boardwalk and approached the two dead men. He studied their faces in the light coming through the saloon windows. After a moment he pointed at one of them. "This man is Carl Jenkins. Several years ago I was trying to arrest his brother Ted. I had to shoot him when he resisted and nearly cut my head off with an ax. There's a resemblance between these two men, so I suspect they're brothers as well. Wouldn't surprise me if the one in the hotel is a Jenkins, too."

Tate had picked a good time to remember things, The Kid thought. His answers sounded utterly convincing, and for all The Kid knew, they were correct.

The second lawman, who was probably a deputy, said, "I think the old-timer's right, Marshal. I've seen this one on a wanted poster. Seem to recall he was wanted for train robbery."

"Ted Jenkins was a train robber, too," Tate said. "It must have been the family business."

The local marshal sighed and nodded to The Kid. "All right, I reckon you can pick up your gun. It's pretty clear these fellas had a revenge killing in mind when they threw down on you. Have they been trailing you?"

"I don't know," The Kid answered honestly. He hadn't been aware anyone was after them, but he supposed it was possible.

Tate had been a lawman for a long time, he reminded himself. Any man who packed a badge and enforced the law was bound to make himself a lot of enemies.

The Kid wondered how many more men were out there who wanted Jared Tate dead.

Chapter 20

The Dodge City marshal, whose name was Thad Hartley, found several people who'd been on the street when the gunfight broke out and who were willing to back up The Kid's story. He had no choice but to consider the killings self-defense.

A hastily assembled coroner's jury rendered the same verdict at a hearing the next morning, so The Kid and Tate were free to go.

They had gone back to the hotel stable and were getting ready to ride when a young man in a brown tweed suit and bowler hat approached them.

"Excuse me," the man said. "Mr. Morgan? Marshal Tate? I was wondering if I might have a few minutes of your time."

The Kid regarded the stranger suspiciously. "We're about to ride out."

"This won't take long," the man assured him. "I just have a few questions."

That confirmed what The Kid's instincts had told him. The man was a newspaper reporter. Back in the days when he was still Conrad Browning, The Kid had had to deal with many of them, and the experiences were nearly always unrewarding and sometimes downright irritating.

"We don't have anything to say." The Kid

179

turned his back to tighten the saddle cinch on his buckskin.

"But you were involved in the biggest gunfight in Dodge City in years and years," the young reporter persisted. "Marshal Tate, surely you can tell me how it felt to be in the middle of such an adventure again, with guns going off and bullets zipping around your head—"

"I told you, no comment," The Kid said as he moved between the reporter and Tate. He fixed the young man with a cold, stony stare.

To the reporter's credit, he didn't back off. "Mr. Morgan, I'm just trying to do my job here."

"And the marshal and I are just trying to go on about our business."

"What business is that? Where are you headed?"

"We're going to Wichita to see my daughter," Tate answered before The Kid could stop him. "And then we're going back to Copperhead Springs. I'm the marshal there, you know."

The Kid tried not to grimace. He wished Tate hadn't said that about Copperhead Springs.

The reporter frowned in confusion. "I thought you'd been retired for several years, Marshal."

"Nonsense," Tate responded without hesitation. "Why in the world would I take off my badge when I'm still perfectly capable of doing the job?"

"But . . . I don't understand . . ."

"Just let it go," The Kid said quietly. "You don't want to write anything about Marshal Tate. There's no story here."

"I'm not so sure about that."

It wouldn't take long for the reporter to look into matters and discover that Tate really was retired and had been for several years, just as he'd thought. Tate's sincere denial of that would be like waving a red flag in front of a bull for a journalist. The reporter would want to know why Tate would say such a thing, and that would lead him straight to Tate's mental problems and inability to remember things.

"Look, I'm asking you, just forget about this," The Kid said. "You won't be doing anybody any good by poking your nose in where it doesn't belong."

"Well, that's sort of my job, Mr. Morgan," the young man insisted.

The Kid's eyes narrowed.

"And . . . and I guess you can shoot me if you want to, I know who you are, you're a gunfighter," the reporter went on nervously. "I can't stop you. But I can't just ignore a story, either."

"It's a story that won't do anybody any good."

"That's not up to you to decide."

It was a losing battle, and The Kid knew it. He couldn't just shoot the reporter . . . although it wasn't a totally unappealing prospect. But they didn't have to wait around and make the young man's job easier. "Come on, Marshal, we've got places to go."

As they mounted up, Tate told the reporter, "You come to Copperhead Springs sometime, young man, and look me up at the marshal's office. I'd be glad to give you an interview for your newspaper."

"Maybe I'll do that, Marshal. Thanks."

The Kid knew he could either get down from his horse and knock the smirk off the reporter's face, or ride away.

He rode away, taking Tate with him and leaving Dodge City behind.

He hoped they weren't leaving a lot of fresh trouble behind as well.

The empty wagon rolled into Dodge City a day later with Selmon handling the reins and Benny riding on the seat beside him. Selmon had wound up trading more of the moonshine to Abner Rutherford for the team, because what good was a wagon without horses to pull it?

The farm where they lived and brewed their hooch was north of there. They didn't try to sell the shine in those parts because the law would crack down on them if they did. Dodge City law didn't care what they did way the hell and gone up in the badlands, though.

"I'll pick up a few supplies, then we'll head out to the farm." Selmon brought the wagon to a halt in front of one of the general stores. He had the money he'd gotten from Rutherford in his pocket, which was good. None of the merchants in Dodge would give him and Benny any credit.

"I'm gonna stay here," Benny said. "My foot still hurts too much to walk on it less'n I have to."

"Fine," Selmon snapped. He was tired of Benny's whining and complaining. He climbed down from the wagon and went into the store.

The place wasn't busy at the moment. The white-haired proprietor was leaning on the counter at the back of the room reading a newspaper. He straightened and set the paper aside when he saw a customer coming, but grunted disdainfully as he recognized Selmon.

"Unless you can pay—"

"I've got money, damn it," Selmon cut in. He took a double eagle from his pocket and slapped it on the counter. "Need some coffee and beans and sugar."

The storekeeper picked up the coin and squinted at it. "Looks real."

"It is real," Selmon said. "Bite it if you don't believe me."

"Considering that it's been in your pocket, I don't believe I will." The storekeeper dropped the coin on the counter again. "I'll gather up your supplies."

"You do that," Selmon said. *One of these days, me and Benny are gonna hit it rich,* he thought, *and then we'll shake the dust of this backwater town off our boots.* It was the same thought that went through his head every time he came to Dodge.

To pass the time while the proprietor was getting the order ready, Selmon picked up the newspaper the man had put aside. He'd had several years of schooling when he was a kid, before he ran away from home, and he'd picked up the knack of reading without much trouble. One of the head-lines caught his eye immediately.

Old-Fashioned Gunfight on Streets of Dodge City

Smaller letters under the headline read: **Famous Lawman Jared Tate Involved in Violent Altercation.**

Selmon's eyes widened as he read the story. It seemed three outlaw brothers—Carl, Jonas, and Lemuel Jenkins—had attacked two visitors to Dodge City, one of whom was retired marshal Jared Tate. When Selmon saw the name Carl, he knew that was the man who'd asked him about Tate at Rutherford's place. It hadn't taken long for Carl and his brothers to catch up to their quarry.

Unfortunately, the three of them had wound up dead, and Tate, along with his traveling companion, a man named Morgan, had come through the fight without a scratch. They had ridden out of

Dodge after being cleared by a coroner's jury, resuming their journey to Wichita.

So siccing Carl on them hadn't done a damn bit of good, Selmon thought bitterly. Tate and that fella Morgan were still out there.

The newspaper story didn't end there. It went on to talk about Jared Tate's illustrious career as a lawman, then described how he had retired—actually, been forced to retire, the way the story had it, Selmon noted with a frown—because of health problems.

The old peckerwood had certainly seemed healthy enough when he was tackling him, Selmon thought. If there was nothing wrong with Tate's body . . . did that mean there was something wrong with his mind?

Wouldn't that just be the biggest joke there was? The famous gunfighting marshal turned addle-brained old geezer? It would mean that fella Morgan wasn't just riding with Tate. He was the old man's keeper.

Pure speculation, Selmon reminded himself. Might not any of it be true.

But it was true Tate and Morgan were still on their way to Wichita, and it was equally true the need for revenge still burned brightly inside Selmon.

"Hold on a minute," he called to the storekeeper. "I'm gonna need more supplies than I thought at first. Plus I need a pistol and one of

185

those Winchester rifles and plenty of ammunition."

That would take all the money he and Benny had, but it didn't matter. Not as long as there was a score to settle.

"What are you gonna do?" the storekeeper asked as he came back to face Selmon across the counter. "Go off and fight a war?"

"Not exactly." Selmon grinned. "But pretty close to it."

Chapter 21

A couple days passed without any trouble, but The Kid didn't let his guard down. He knew that for all of its vastness, the West was a small place in some ways. News traveled faster than seemed possible. If word got around that Tate was on his way to Wichita, more enemies from his past might show up.

If that blasted reporter put anything in his story about the marshal's mental problems, likely it would draw more vultures who wanted to pick at the old lawman's carcass.

After several days of being fairly sharp, Tate's mind had retreated into the past again. Half the time he didn't know who The Kid was, where they were, or where they were going. But at least he hadn't tried to get his hands on a gun and kill "Brick Cantrell" again.

They came to a crossroads with several signs nailed to a post. Tate reined in and pointed to one of the signs, an arrow pointing north that read CHALK BUTTE. "I know that name. Why is the name of that place familiar to me?"

The Kid thought for a moment before he recalled the first night he and Tate had been together on the trail, before they ever reached Copperhead Springs. "That's where Bob Porter is from. You remember him, Marshal?"

"Porter . . . Porter . . . Is he a lawman?"

The Kid nodded. "That's right. He was after those men who tried to kill me and steal my horse. You came along and gave me a hand, otherwise I'd have wound up dead. That's how we met."

Tate smiled slightly and shook his head. "If you say so. I'm afraid I don't remember that, Kid."

"Porter said for us to stop by for a visit if we were ever in his neck of the woods," The Kid mused. He thought about how tired and haggard Tate was looking. With the man's mental problems, it was easy to forget he was getting on in years and no longer had the strength and stamina he had once possessed. Stopping to let him rest for a day or two might not be a bad idea.

"Why don't we go see him?" The Kid went on, hoping Tate would agree with the suggestion. He didn't want to have to argue with the old lawman.

"That's fine," Tate said dully. "Whatever you want."

His attitude was worrisome. He seemed to be sinking into despair. It would be hard not to feel like that at times, The Kid thought. Even though Tate's mind was too fuzzy to understand, he had to be aware that something was wrong with him, had to know he was no longer the man he had been. That would weigh on anybody.

The Kid turned his buckskin onto the trail leading north, and Tate followed suit. The sign didn't indicate how many miles it was to Chalk Butte, but The Kid hoped they could reach the settlement before nightfall.

Like Dodge City, Abilene was long past its glory days. A lot of people living in Abilene didn't have any memory of the time when Wild Bill Hickok had been the city marshal, when vast herds of cattle had been driven up the trail by armies of wild Texas cowboys, when Front Street had been lined with saloons roaring with life twenty-four hours a day. All that had gone when the railhead had moved on, leaving a sleepy, dusty community where a church social was considered excitement.

After years in prison, it was just the sort of place Brick Cantrell was looking for. Nobody in Abilene would be expecting trouble. It would be easy pickings.

He rode up to the train station and reined in, a big, rawboned man with a thatch of once red hair that was now mostly gray. As he swung down from the saddle he glanced along the street, noting the positions of the other members of the gang he had put together since being released a couple months earlier. This would be their first job but far from their last, Cantrell told himself. Soon his name would be as known—and as feared—throughout Kansas as it had been ten years earlier.

He was sure most people had expected him never to see the outside of a prison again. Funny how things hadn't worked out that way. The army had kept him in the stockade for a year for desertion, and then he'd been dishonorably discharged and transferred to the state penitentiary to serve a nine-year sentence for armed robbery. While it was true people had been killed during the crimes his gang had committed he had never killed anyone. He'd had a good lawyer, too. So he didn't swing, and he hadn't been sentenced to life in prison.

Some folks were going to be mighty surprised when they heard about that. The thought brought a grin to Cantrell's ugly face as he walked into the depot.

Since being released, he hadn't had any trouble putting together a gang. Some of the men who'd ridden with him were still around, and others were eager to partner up with the notorious Brick Cantrell. At the moment, he had fifteen men on the street, ready to move on his signal. Some would drift into the depot before the train arrived. They would help him take over, loot the express car, and rob the passengers. The others would surround the station and keep the townspeople from interfering, if anybody was foolhardy enough to try such a thing.

A few people were inside the depot, either waiting for someone to come in on the train or there to board themselves. None of them paid any attention to Cantrell.

They would pay attention to him soon enough, Cantrell thought. There would be screams of fear, too, just the sort of music he liked.

A glance at the chalkboard next to the ticket window told him the eastbound was on schedule. He took out his pocket watch and flipped it open. Another fifteen minutes or so and the train would arrive.

Another fifteen minutes and Brick Cantrell's second career as an outlaw would be launched.

In the meantime, he sat down on one of the benches to wait and idly picked up a newspaper some traveler had left behind. A headline about a gunfight caught his eye.

The Dodge City paper from a few days earlier crinkled as his hands tightened on it. A familiar name leaped from the densely printed paragraphs.

Jared Tate.

Tate. The man who had captured him. The man responsible for the past ten years behind bars.

The man Brick Cantrell hated more than anyone else in the world.

He stood up, folded the paper, and stuck it under his arm. The man he had settled on to be second in command, Herb Tuttle, had just come into the depot. Cantrell caught his eye and stalked toward him.

"What's up, Brick?" Tuttle asked. "I thought we were gonna pretend not to know each other until the train got here."

"Forget the damned train," Cantrell snapped. "There's something more important I have to do first."

"More important than a job?"

Cantrell showed him the paper, stabbing a blunt finger down on the story about Marshal Jared Tate. "This is the hombre who put me behind bars. According to this story, he's headed in this direction. He hasn't had time to get here from Dodge yet."

"Wait a minute." Tuttle frowned as he scanned the printed lines. "Wichita's southeast of here. He wouldn't be coming exactly this way."

"I know. That's why we've got to cut him off."

Tuttle hesitated, then said, "Look, Brick, I understand you've got a score to settle with this lawdog, but we put some planning into this job. The boys are counting on the loot they'll get from it."

"There'll be other trains we can hold up,"

Cantrell snapped, "and plenty of loot later on. Tate's old, and this story makes him sound like he's sick. I can't let the old peckerwood die before I come face-to-face with him again."

"Seems like you'd want him dead, after what he did to you."

"I do . . . but I've got to be the one who kills him." With a vicious snap of his wrist, Cantrell threw the folded newspaper into a nearby wastebasket. "Get out there and spread the word to the rest of the boys. We're callin' off this job, and heading south to intercept Tate and this fella Morgan who's riding with him. If they don't like it, they can do whatever they damn well please, but they won't be riding with Brick Cantrell anymore."

"Take it easy, Brick, take it easy," Tuttle urged. He sighed. "We'll go along with you . . . for now. But once this chore is done, we'll be expecting to clean up on the next job."

"Sure. I'll even forgo my share, to make up for calling off this job." Cantrell heard a train whistle in the distance. "Better hurry, Herb. Get the boys together. We'll rendezvous south of town."

Tuttle nodded and hurried out of the depot. Cantrell started to follow him, then detoured to stand for a moment in front of a large map of Kansas tacked to one of the station walls.

His eyes traced the route Tate and Morgan would take from Dodge City to Wichita. He tried to estimate the amount of ground they could have covered in the time since they'd left Dodge on horseback. If Tate was in poor health, as the newspaper story made it sound, surely they couldn't travel too fast. There was still time for Cantrell and his men to get in front of them.

A good trail led in the right direction. It passed through several small settlements along the way: Hope Corners, Friedlander, Chalk Butte.

Maybe once he was finished with Tate, the gang could raid one of those towns and empty it of everything valuable, just as the Cantrell gang had done in the old days. It might be enough to appease any hard feelings left over from calling off the train robbery.

To tell the truth, Brick Cantrell didn't really care, one way or the other. He just wanted his revenge on Jared Tate.

Once he had that, everything else would take care of itself.

Chapter 22

It was pretty obvious where the town of Chalk Butte got its name. The landmark in question rose about half a mile west of the settlement. It wasn't very tall, thirty or forty feet, but on the Kansas plains even that much height made it stand out.

The town itself was about half the size of

Copperhead Springs, The Kid thought as he and Tate rode in. A pleasant enough place with a main street a few blocks long, a couple white-washed churches with tall steeples, and a red-brick schoolhouse at the edge of town.

At least, it would have been pleasant if something wasn't wrong. The Kid's eyes narrowed as he realized no one was on the streets. No teams and wagons were parked in front of the stores, and no horses were tied at the hitch racks. All the doors were closed.

From the looks of it, Chalk Butte had been abandoned.

Even Tate could see and understand that. "Where is everybody?"

"I don't know, Marshal," The Kid answered quietly. "I sure don't like the looks of this."

The sound of a door opening made him stiffen in the saddle. He turned quickly in the direction of the sound, his hand moving toward his Colt.

"Hold it, mister!" a voice called sharply. The Kid found himself looking over the barrel of a rifle aimed at him from a doorway. Instinct made him glance along the street. Other rifles had appeared, thrust from doors and windows.

Keeping his voice strong and steady, The Kid said, "Take it easy, friend. We're not looking for trouble."

A few heartbeats of silence ticked by.

"Good Lord. It's Marshal Tate and Mr. Morgan."

The door swung back, and Marshal Bob Porter stepped out of the building. He lowered his rifle and waved a hand over his head in a signal that everything was all right.

"What in the world's going on here?" The Kid asked without making a move to dismount.

"The town's waiting for trouble," Porter said in his Texas drawl.

"I can see that. What kind of trouble?"

"The Boomhauser brothers. Three old buffalo hunters. I had to arrest one of them the other night for raising a ruckus in one of the saloons. He paid his fine for disturbing the peace, so I didn't have any choice but to let him go. He said he was going to get his brothers and come back to teach the town a lesson."

Tate blew out a disgusted sigh. "There's always something like that going on when you're a lawman. Folks just won't accept it when they're wrong and let things go."

"The Boomhausers won't, that's for sure. They've treed other towns and gotten away with it. That's not going to happen here."

"And you're expecting them any time now."

Porter nodded. "Yep."

Someone else stepped out of the building, which The Kid finally recognized as the marshal's office and jail. His eyebrows rose as he realized the newcomer was a young woman, despite the fact that she wore boots, whipcord trousers, and a short charro jacket over a silk shirt. She had a Winchester in her hands and a gun belt strapped around her trim hips.

"You know these men, Papa?" she asked.

"Yeah." Porter inclined his head toward her and went on. "My daughter Holly."

With her olive skin, dark eyes, and mass of raven-black hair, Holly Porter was beautiful. She handled the rifle like she knew how to use it, and The Kid felt another jolt of surprise when he saw the badge pinned to her jacket.

"Your daughter is your deputy?" he asked.

Porter grinned. "She comes from good fighting stock on both sides. Why not?"

Tate pursed his lips in obvious disapproval. "I never heard of such a thing. A woman can't be a deputy."

"Remember how Constance was right in the middle of the fight with the Broken Spoke?" The Kid said. "She was as much a part of that as anybody else."

"Maybe so," Tate said grudgingly, "but some things just don't seem right to me."

"We need to get off the street," Porter said. "When the Boomhausers get here, they're liable to come in shooting. I don't want anybody to get hurt. There's a little corral out back. You can put your horses there."

The Kid and Tate dismounted and led the animals around the building. Porter opened the rear door to let them in that way after they had put the horses in the corral and unsaddled them.

"You fellas might have preferred to just ride on," he commented once they were inside. "This isn't your trouble, after all. You already helped me out once when you took care of those outlaws I was after."

"And you said then to stop by and pay you a visit sometime." The Kid smiled. "That's why we're here." He leaned his head toward Tate and lowered his voice. "And to let the marshal rest a little before we head on to Wichita."

Porter's eyes narrowed slightly as he studied Tate. "Is something the matter with . . . No, never mind. We can talk about that later."

The Kid nodded in agreement.

Somewhere outside, a bell began to ring. Porter and his daughter looked around, their heads jerking toward the sound. Obviously, they knew what the signal meant.

"We've got a man in the bell tower of the Methodist Church," Porter said. "He's warning us the Boomhausers are on their way."

The marshal took a step toward the door.

Holly caught the sleeve of his buckskin jacket and stopped him. "You can't go out there by yourself, Papa. I'm going with you."

Porter shook his head. "Not hardly. You can cover me from the window, but you're not setting foot outside this building, Holly. I already let you run enough risks just wearing that badge. You want your mama to turn all the way over in her grave?"

"My mother would be the first one to back you up in case of trouble," Holly said, her voice fiery with anger and determination.

"Well, that's true enough, I reckon. But you're still not—"

"I'll come with you, Marshal," The Kid said.

Porter looked at him with narrowed eyes. "You're not even a lawman, Mr. Morgan. It's not your job—"

"I'm volunteering," The Kid cut in. "If Miss Porter—I mean Deputy Porter—can keep an eye on Marshal Tate for me, I'd be glad to help you out."

"Nobody needs to keep an eye on me," Tate said. "I'm fine."

"I want you to stay here anyway, Marshal," The Kid said. "As a favor to me."

Tate sighed and nodded. "All right. But I get tired of being treated like I'm five years old."

The Kid wished that wasn't necessary. For now, he had more pressing concerns.

"You want a rifle?" Porter asked as they moved toward the door, not giving Holly the chance to continue the argument.

"No, my Colt ought to be enough. How many of these Boomhausers are there?"

"Just three." a grim smile curved Porter's

mouth. "But they're about as big and tough as the buffalo they used to hunt."

The two men stepped out onto the porch. Before Porter closed the door behind them, The Kid glanced through the opening and saw the angry, frustrated face of Holly. The emotions she was feeling didn't make her any less beautiful, he noted.

Three men on horseback had entered the town. Even from a distance of several blocks, The Kid could tell how big they were. The horses they rode stood tall, but in comparison to the riders the animals looked a bit like ponies.

Despite the warmth of the day, all three men wore buffalo coats, which made them look even bigger. As The Kid studied the massive, shaggy figures, he said quietly to Porter, "I see what you mean about them. Buffalo walking on two legs."

"Damn near," Porter agreed. "You sure you want to take cards in this game, Morgan?"

"I'd say the hand's already been dealt."

The Kid and Porter moved slowly into the middle of the deserted street. In a low voice, Porter said, "That's Alvin on our left, Hubert in the middle, and Forrest on the right."

"How do you tell 'em apart?" The Kid wanted to know. The faces of all three men bristled with beards.

"Alvin's the good-looking one," Porter replied with a dry chuckle.

"I'll have to take your word for that." The Kid grinned.

As the Boomhausers came on at a slow, deliberate pace The Kid continued, "All the big herds have been gone for a long time. What have these boys been doing since then?"

"They have a farm north of here. Most of the time they're not bad sorts, really, but when they get to drinking . . . That's what happened with Hubert the other day. He just can't hold his liquor, and neither can the other two."

"As big as they are, they ought to be able to down a whole barrel of whiskey without feeling it."

"You'd think so, but it doesn't always work out that way." Porter licked dry lips. "Times like this, I almost wish I was back on the Rio Grande."

The Kid didn't really believe that. Porter seemed calm and confident, not the least bit spooked by the dangerous confrontation.

The Boomhausers brought their horses to a halt about twenty feet from the two men standing in the street. Hubert, the one in the middle, leaned forward and said in a voice that rumbled like distant thunder, "I told you I'd be back with my brothers, Marshal. You had no call to arrest me."

"You were drunk and causing damage in the saloon, Hubert," Porter said. "I was afraid you were going to hurt somebody, and I knew you wouldn't want that."

"I'm gonna hurt somebody, all right. You." Hubert glared at The Kid. "And who's that spindly young fella with you?"

"This is a friend of mine, Kid Morgan."

"Well, Kid, you better light a shuck while you still can if you don't want part of the marshal's trouble. Consider that fair warnin'."

"And consider *this* fair warning, Mr. Boomhauser," The Kid said right back. "You're not going to cause trouble here today. Turn around and ride out."

The one called Alvin shifted in his saddle. "Is this stranger givin' the orders now, Marshal?"

"Morgan wants the same thing I do," Porter snapped. "No bloodshed. Listen, you three . . . there are a dozen rifles covering you right now. You might manage to kill the two of us, but you'll be shot to pieces if you do. I don't want anybody hurt, including you."

"It don't matter," Hubert insisted. "We been insulted. Somebody's got to pay."

"Would you consider the chance for a fair fight payment enough?" The Kid suddenly asked.

Porter glanced over at him and muttered, "What're you doing, Morgan?"

The Kid reached down to his gun belt and started to unbuckle it. "You and I will take each other on, Hubert, how about that? And when the fight's over, win, lose, or draw, you and your brothers turn around, ride back to your farm, and promise to stop causing trouble around here."

"You're loco!" Hubert exclaimed.

"My brother can bust you in half with one hand!" Alvin added.

Porter said, "They're right, Morgan. You wouldn't stand a chance against that behemoth."

"But if they'll go along with the deal, then nobody has to die today," The Kid pointed out.

"Except maybe you."

"I'll be all right."

Hubert clawed fingers through his beard and looked back and forth at his brothers. "What do you reckon I ought to do?"

"That's up to you," Alvin said.

Forrest Boomhauser spoke for the first time. "Rip the scrawny little varmint to pieces."

Hubert nodded. "All right," he declared. "We'll fight it out, me and this stranger, and that'll be the end of it. But if he winds up dead, Marshal, you can't blame me and call it murder."

"Nobody's going to do that," The Kid said before Porter could respond. "It's a fair fight, nothing more than that." He handed his gun belt and hat to Porter. "Hang on to these for me, will you, Marshal?"

"Sure, but I'm afraid you won't be needing 'em anymore."

"We'll see." The Kid rolled up the sleeves of his shirt.

Hubert Boomhauser dismounted and stepped

away from his horse. He handed his gun and hat to his brother Alvin.

"Aren't you going to take that buffalo coat off?" The Kid asked.

"I don't like to," Hubert said. "That make any difference to you?"

"I suppose not," The Kid replied with a shake of his head. "Whenever you're—"

Before he could say "ready," Hubert charged him with a deafening roar.

To The Kid it felt like the very earth was shaking under his feet . . . as if a whole herd of buffalo was stampeding straight at him.

<u>Chapter 23</u>

Alvin and Forrest Boomhauser let out excited yells. Marshal Porter shouted, "Look out, Morgan!" and The Kid thought he heard a frightened, feminine cry come from Holly inside the marshal's office.

But none of those things mattered. Facing a monster like Hubert, he couldn't let himself be distracted if he wanted to stay alive.

He twisted aside and threw himself out of Hubert's path. Clubbing his hands together, he swung them in a smashing blow to the back of Hubert's neck as he lumbered past. The Kid put all his strength behind the punch.

Hubert didn't even seem to feel it.

He wheeled around ponderously, swinging a massive arm in a backhand. Although bigger than Jed Ahern, whom The Kid had battled back in Copperhead Springs, he lacked Ahern's surprising speed. The Kid was able to drop under that sweeping arm without any trouble.

Sometimes a big man would have a glass jaw, or his nose would be his weak spot. The Kid darted in and hammered a short left and right into the middle of Hubert's face.

Hubert's head didn't rock back even an inch under the impact of the blows.

The Kid jumped back, escaping Hubert's attempt to grab him in a bear hug. He wasn't a dirty fighter by nature, but he gave some thought to kicking Hubert in the groin. Nothing else seemed to be doing any good.

Let that be a last resort, The Kid decided. He bored in again, sending a pile driver punch at Hubert's head.

Capable of some speed, after all, Hubert got his hand up and grabbed The Kid's wrist before the blow could land. He turned and heaved . . .

And suddenly The Kid found himself airborne.

He landed in the middle of the street, where his momentum sent him rolling over and over. As dust billowed up around him, choking him and making him cough, he realized Hubert had flung him through the air like a child throwing a rag doll.

It was like fighting a mountain on legs.

The Kid did some quick calculations. If he could keep Hubert from smashing his skull in or breaking his back, maybe he could outlast the former buffalo hunter. Hubert was considerably older than him. Not as old as Tate, certainly, but The Kid still had the advantage in years. Hubert might get tired.

The ground was shaking again. The Kid looked up and saw Hubert barreling at him like a runaway freight train. He scrambled up onto hands and knees, and launched himself forward, throwing his body right into Hubert's knees.

The impact was tremendous, jolting The Kid to the core of his being, but he'd finally done some damage. With a startled yell, Hubert plunged forward out of control as The Kid knocked his legs out from under him. He went down like an avalanche.

Grimacing from the pain of having Hubert's knees rammed into his torso, The Kid rolled over and got to his feet. Seeing Hubert was still down, The Kid leaped on him, landing with his knees in the small of the big man's back.

Again he clubbed his hands together and hammered them against the back of Hubert's head. The powerful blow drove Hubert's face into the dirt. The Kid raised his arms and brought them down a second time.

Hubert roared and came to his feet, almost

straight up. The Kid nearly fell off, but lunged forward and got his arms around Hubert's neck. In spite of the thick beard and buffalo coat in his way, he managed to thrust his right forearm across Hubert's throat and grab that wrist with his left hand to lock it down

Hubert tried to bellow again but The Kid cut off his air. He clawed at The Kid's arm. His thick, blunt fingers couldn't get inside the smaller man's grip and tear it loose.

The Kid's feet dangled well off the ground as he hung on for dear life. Hubert turned around and around, trying to sling him off. But The Kid didn't let go.

Suddenly Hubert stopped spinning and lurched backward.

The Kid realized his opponent was trying to smash him against a building. He twisted his head around to glance back at the wall rushing toward him.

Timing the move perfectly, he let go and dropped right behind Hubert. The big man tripped over him and crashed into the wall with such force that boards splintered under his weight and he knocked a hole in the wall. Stunned, he fell through the opening, his legs still draped across The Kid.

Fighting down a touch of panic, The Kid struggled out from under them. He made it to his feet and turned to see that Hubert wasn't moving.

For a moment he thought the man had fatally impaled himself on a broken board or something, but as the pounding of his own pulse subsided, he heard the rasp of the big man's breathing.

"Is he still alive?" one of his brothers called anxiously.

The Kid turned away from the scene of destruction and nodded. "He's alive. Looks like he knocked himself out when he ran through the wall."

"That was a dirty trick," the other Boomhauser brother accused.

"I didn't hear anything about any damned Marquis of Queensbury rules," The Kid snapped. "As far as I know, it was no holds barred and devil take the hindmost."

"That *is* the way Hubert always fought," Alvin said.

"Yeah, I reckon so," Forrest agreed grudgingly. "But I still say that little fella couldn't 'a beat him without cheatin' somehow."

Porter said, "It was a fair fight. Everybody in town saw that. And you know good and well Hubert would be the first one to agree with that. He said he wanted a fair fight in return for being arrested, and he got one. Now you boys pick him up and get out of town, and don't come back until you're ready to not cause any more trouble."

"Deal's a deal," Alvin said heavily. "That fella's mighty lucky Hubert didn't kill him, though."

"Looked more like good smart fighting to me," Porter said.

The brothers dismounted, went over to Hubert, and dragged him out of the hole in the wrecked wall.

"We ain't payin' for this damage," Forrest said.

"I'll take care of it," The Kid said. "I won, so it's only fair."

Both brothers glared at him, but neither said anything else. Hubert was starting to come to, but he was so groggy he didn't know what was going on. They got him onto his horse, and all three of them rode out of Chalk Butte.

The Kid started brushing dust off his clothes.

Porter looked at him and shook his head. "I hate to agree with the Boomhauser brothers about anything, but I'm mighty surprised you're still alive, Mr. Morgan."

The Kid managed to smile. "They were right about me being lucky."

The door of the marshal's office opened, and Holly walked out, followed by Jared Tate.

"You're one loco hombre," she told The Kid. "But it looks like you saved us from having to bury anybody today."

"I knew you could beat him," Tate said. "Never had a doubt in my mind."

"I appreciate that, Marshal," The Kid said.

Up and down the street, people were starting to emerge from the buildings.

Porter called to them, "It's all right, folks! The trouble's over!" He turned back to the other three. "Maybe now things can get back to normal around here."

Marshal Porter and his daughter lived in a small but neat house around the corner from the jail. With no extra room for The Kid and Tate to stay there, they got rooms in Chalk Butte's only hotel. It was fine with The Kid. He hadn't wanted to put them out, anyway.

Porter insisted they come to the house for supper, however, and the two travelers were happy to accept that invitation.

Holly prepared enchiladas, a stew peppery enough to take the breath away, beans, and tortillas. The Kid hadn't spent much time on the Mexican border, but when Porter made the comment the food was like what they ate along the Rio Grande, The Kid believed it.

"Holly comes by her cooking skills honestly. Her mother was the sister of an old trail pard of mine," Porter explained. Her family had a big rancho just on the other side of the border from the ranch that my folks owned."

"How about my gun-handling skills?" Holly asked with a smile. "Do I come by those honestly, too?"

"I'm afraid you do," Porter said. "That's about all you got from me, though. Your looks and that temper of yours, those are all your mother's."

Holly tossed her head as if to prove her father's point.

When the meal was finished, the men took cups of coffee out to the front porch to enjoy the evening air. Tate sat down in a rocking chair. Porter and The Kid stood at the railing, looking over the street.

"You say you're on your way to Wichita?" Porter asked.

"That's right," The Kid said. "We're going to visit Marshal Tate's daughter."

"Well, that's a good thing. If Holly didn't live here, I'd sure want to go visit her from time to time." Porter lowered his voice and went on. "To tell you the truth, I hope she doesn't spend the rest of her life here. She was always a tomboy, but being a deputy marshal's no kind of way for a young woman to live. She needs a husband, and kids of her own."

"Maybe that's the way it'll turn out," The Kid said. "I've found that fate usually has its own plans for us, though, and those don't always turn out the way we might hope."

"I suppose that's true."

A snore came from Tate as he leaned back in the rocking chair. The Kid reached over, gently took the half-empty coffee cup from the old lawman's hand, and set it on the porch railing.

"Poor old fella's worn out," Porter said quietly.

"It's been less than a month since I saw you boys that other time, and Marshal Tate looks like he's aged a year in that time."

"Some days are better than others for him," The Kid explained. "You're right, though. The trip's been hard on him, and it hasn't helped that we've run into trouble several times along the way. I'll be glad to get him back to Wichita so his daughter can look after him."

"This isn't just a visit you're going on, is it?"

The Kid shook his head. "The marshal's mind isn't right anymore. Some days he knows where he is and what's going on, but most of the time he doesn't really remember. He thinks it's ten or fifteen years ago and he's still the marshal of Copperhead Springs."

"I knew that couldn't be right when he mentioned it before," Porter said. "I've heard about people like that who get really confused when they're older. Doesn't seem like there's anything that can be done about it."

"There isn't," The Kid agreed. "At least not that I know of."

"You just have to take care of them and make sure they don't hurt themselves or other folks."

"That's right." The Kid paused, then went on. "I had to take his gun away from him when he almost shot me one morning. Seems he'd convinced himself I was his old enemy Brick Cantrell."

"Cantrell . . ." Porter repeated. "I know that name."

"He was an army deserter and outlaw. Marshal Tate put him behind bars ten years ago. I suppose he's still there."

"More than likely. Seems I remember hearing something about him. . . ." Porter shook his head. "I can't recall what it was, though. Don't reckon it matters anyway. Those days are long behind Marshal Tate now."

"That's right. From here on out somebody needs to see to it that he's cared for and comfortable." The Kid wouldn't have said it if Tate had been awake, but he added, "Jared Tate's outlaw-fighting days are done."

Chapter 24

Herb Tuttle had been right about the other members of the gang being upset because Cantrell called off the train robbery in Abilene at the last minute, but there were enough old-timers in the group still loyal to him to offset the young firebrands who might have said the gang needed a new leader.

Cantrell had pushed them hard, not wanting Tate and Morgan to get past him. He would trail Tate all the way to Wichita to get his revenge if he had to, but it would be easier if the gang didn't have to venture into the city.

They had skirted around the smaller settlements on their way south, but supplies were running low and Cantrell knew he ought to send a couple men into the next town they came to. As the riders, almost two dozen strong, approached the place called Chalk Butte, Cantrell signaled a halt and waved Tuttle up alongside him.

"Take one of the men and ride into town, Herb. The rest of us will swing west around that butte and wait on the far side of it."

"What is it you want me to do?" Tuttle asked. "Pick up some provisions? I know we're runnin' a little low."

"That's right." Cantrell gave him some money. "Get enough to last us several days."

Tuttle frowned slightly. "The storekeeper's liable to wonder why two men are buyin' so many supplies."

"Let him wonder," Cantrell snapped. "When you put cash on the barrelhead, he's not going to care too much."

"Yeah, you're probably right about that," Tuttle said with a chuckle. "Never saw a storekeeper yet who cared about much of anything except makin' money."

Tuttle picked the outlaw named Rowden to go with him. They split off from the other men and rode toward the settlement while Cantrell led the rest of the gang toward the butte.

As they jogged along on their horses, Rowden

said, "A lot of the boys still ain't happy about this wild goose chase, Herb. I thought this would be a good chance to say something about that to you, since you and Cantrell are close. Maybe you can talk some sense into his head. We didn't sign on to settle no personal grudge."

Tuttle looked over at the other man and asked coolly, "Are you done?"

"Well . . . yeah, I reckon so."

"Then let me tell you something. You're one of the fellas who never rode with Brick before, so you don't really know what you're talkin' about. He led the gang for several years, and he never steered us wrong."

Rowden looked like he didn't want to argue, but he said, "Then how come Cantrell wound up in prison and the rest of the gang got busted up?"

"That was just pure bad luck," Tuttle snapped. "Bad luck, and that damned Marshal Tate bein' more stubborn than any lawman had a right to be. Most star packers would've given up before they chased us down like that. I don't blame Brick for hatin' Tate and wantin' to settle the score with him. Once that's done, you'll see what sort of gang this really is."

"Well, if you say so, Herb. But I hope it don't take too long to find this Tate. If it does, some of the boys might start thinkin' they ought to go off on their own."

"They'd be sorry if they ever did," Tuttle said.

They left it at that, because they were getting close to the settlement. Chalk Butte wasn't a very big town, but it was big enough to have a general store where they could buy the supplies they needed.

A few minutes later they reined to a halt in front of the mercantile and swung down from their saddles. Tuttle led the way as they went up the steps to the porch and then inside the building.

Because he was in front, he saw the girl first, and she was stunning enough to make him stop short. She was dressed like a man in high boots, whipcord trousers, and a buckskin shirt, but there was no doubt she was female. The curves displayed by the outfit were ample proof of that.

Rowden bumped into Tuttle's back. "What the hell? Why you stop so sudden, Herb?"

Tuttle moved aside slightly so Rowden could see past him. That was all it took to answer the question.

The young woman was standing at the counter talking to the storekeeper. She glanced over her shoulder at the newcomers, but didn't really pay any attention to them. It was enough for Tuttle to get a glimpse of her face past the thick, curly black hair. She was every bit as pretty as he expected her to be.

"Good Lord!" Rowden muttered. "I haven't seen a girl who looks like that in, well, maybe ever!"

"Yeah, I know," Tuttle said as he got control of his own reaction to the girl's beauty. "But we're here to buy supplies, not to go courtin', so just forget about her."

"Hell, what harm would it do just to talk to her a little?"

"If you were older, you'd understand. Don't let yourself get distracted from the job you're supposed to do, no matter how good-lookin' the distraction might be. Come on, and keep your mouth shut. You let me do the talkin'."

Rowden muttered some more, but didn't say anything loud enough for Tuttle to understand him as they walked along the store's center aisle toward the counter at the back.

The young woman moved aside when they got there so they could talk to the proprietor. She must have been shooting the breeze with the man and not buying anything, Tuttle thought.

The middle-aged storekeeper put his hands flat on the counter and asked, "Something I can do for you fellas?"

"Yeah, we need some supplies." Tuttle started naming off the items and the amount he wanted to buy.

The storekeeper frowned. "That's a lot of provisions for two men."

"We're travelin' with a few pards who didn't come into town," Tuttle explained. "And we don't like to stop for supplies that often."

216

The storekeeper shrugged. "None of my business. You want these things crated or bagged?"

"Better bag 'em," Tuttle said. "We don't have a wagon, so we'll have to pack 'em on our horses."

"All right. Shouldn't take me long to gather up what you need."

"You're not very busy today," Tuttle commented. He and Rowden were the only customers in the store.

"It's a slack time," the proprietor said with a shrug. "Tomorrow's Saturday. I'll be doing a booming business all day."

Tuttle nodded. Tomorrow at the end of the day would be the best time to rob the store, he thought, since the place would have taken in a lot of cash during the day. Of course, it was just habit that he considered such things, since he and the others would be long gone by then. Once a thief, always a thief, he supposed.

He suddenly became aware that Rowden wasn't standing at his elbow anymore. Looking around in alarm, he saw the younger outlaw sidling up to the woman, who was looking at a display of dresses.

"Damn it, Rowden," Tuttle said under his breath. "Why can't you just listen—"

"Howdy," Rowden said to the young woman. "One of those dresses would look mighty nice on you, ma'am."

She turned her head to look at him and asked coolly, "Do I know you?"

Rowden took his hat off and shook his head. "No, ma'am, I'm just passin' through here, but I have sort of a rule in my life that says never pass up the chance to get to know a beautiful woman, because you never know when you'll run into another one."

Tuttle came up behind him as Rowden was spouting that stuff. "Rowden, come on. Leave the lady alone."

"He's not bothering me," the young woman said with a trace of amusement in her voice. "That would take more than some smooth-talking saddle tramp."

Rowden's forehead creased in a frown. "Now wait just a minute. I'm not exactly a saddle tramp, and I don't like bein' made sport of."

"Then you should be more careful who you try to flirt with," the young woman said.

Tuttle took hold of Rowden's arm. "Come on." He tried to tug Rowden back toward the counter.

"Damn it, Herb!" Rowden pulled away, violently enough so his arm swung around . . .

And hit the young woman across the face, knocking her right into the dress display.

"Son of a— Look what you did!" Tuttle exclaimed as the young woman caught her balance and righted herself.

"Ma'am, I'm sorry. I never meant to—"

Rowden's hurried apology stopped short as he stared at the young woman. She had turned toward them and dropped her hand to the butt of the revolver holstered at her hip. A deputy's badge gleamed where it was pinned to the soft buckskin shirt.

"She's the law!" Rowden said, and as Tuttle watched in horror, instinct sent the young outlaw's hand flashing toward his gun.

The Kid, Jared Tate, and Marshal Porter were walking casually along the street when Porter nodded toward the two men who had just dismounted in front of the general store. "Strangers. Wonder if they're just passing through."

"You try to keep up with all the strangers who come into your town, Marshal?" The Kid asked.

Instead of letting Porter answer for himself, Tate said, "Of course he does. That's part of a lawman's job. Am I right, Marshal?"

"You are correct, Marshal," Porter replied with a grin.

"Those two had the look of hardcases about them, too," Tate went on.

"I was thinking the same thing," Porter agreed. "Maybe we'll mosey in that direction and have a talk with them."

Tate nodded. "An excellent idea."

It seemed more like an overreaction to The Kid. But he wasn't a lawman, he reminded himself.

Anyway, Tate seemed a little more animated than usual by the prospect, so he supposed it wouldn't hurt anything.

Porter didn't get in any hurry to reach the store, stopping to pass the time of day with several citizens along the way. The Kid half expected to see the two men come back out and go on about their business before he and Porter and Tate got there.

They hadn't emerged from the store as The Kid and the two lawmen approached the door, however. Porter went in first, followed by Tate, and then The Kid bringing up the rear.

The Kid heard what sounded like angry voices, then somebody yelled, "She's the law!"

Porter shouted, "Holly!" and lunged forward, clawing at the gun on his hip.

The Kid surged ahead and shouldered Tate out of the line of fire as he palmed out his Colt.

Holly was confronting the two strangers. The younger one had his gun out.

She struck with blinding speed, grabbing the wrist of the stranger's gun hand and thrusting it upward. The gun roared, but the bullet went harmlessly into the ceiling, scattering plaster.

At the same time, the edge of Holly's other hand slashed across the man's throat. He staggered back a step, gasping for breath.

Before he could do anything else, Porter stepped in and slammed the barrel of his gun across the man's head, dropping him senseless to the floor.

The troublemaker's older companion had his hand on the butt of his gun, but he froze with it there as The Kid covered him and said quietly, "I wouldn't do that, mister."

Carefully, the man took his hand away from his gun and raised it along with his other hand. "Take it easy, friend. We're not lookin' for trouble."

"You've got a funny way of doing it," Porter snapped, "trying to take a shot at my deputy . . . and my daughter!"

"We didn't know. Look, this is all just a misunderstanding. My friend here . . . well, I'll admit he was flirtin' with the lady, but he didn't mean any harm. It was just some harmless joshin'."

"He hit me!" Holly had drawn her gun as well.

"That was an accident," the older stranger said. "I had hold of my pard and was tryin' to steer him away, and when he pulled loose he sort of bumped the lady." He looked around at the proprietor of the store. "Tell them, mister. You saw the whole thing. You know it was just an accident."

"It didn't look like he did it on purpose, Marshal," the storekeeper said. "I'll admit that much. And before that these two gents hadn't caused any problems."

Holly asked sharply, "Why did he try to draw on me when he saw my badge?"

The older man sighed and shook his head. "I'll

admit, we've had our share of run-ins with the law. Reckon he just acted without thinking. But we're not wanted, I swear, and we just needed to pick up some supplies and be on our way."

Porter looked at the storekeeper. "How about that, Norman?"

"They were buying supplies, all right. A pretty good lot of them."

Porter thought about it for a moment and then holstered his gun. He said to the older man, "You think you can get him on his feet and get him out of here once you've got your provisions?"

"I'm sure I can, Marshal," the man replied.

"All right. We'll let this go, then, providing both of you get out of town and don't show your faces here again." Porter glanced at Holly. "If that's all right with you. You're the one who got hit."

"It didn't amount to anything," she said with a shrug. "I've had horses bump into me a lot harder. Sure, let 'em go."

She slid her revolver back into its holster, as did The Kid.

"I'm going to keep an eye on them until they ride out of town, though," Holly added.

"That's fine." Porter turned to The Kid. "Thanks for your help, Mr. Morgan."

"I didn't do anything," The Kid said.

"Yeah, but you were ready to step in if you needed to." Porter turned to Tate. "And you were right, as usual, Marshal Tate."

"Well, you pick up some instincts when you wear a badge long enough," the old lawman said.

The three of them started out of the store to continue their stroll around town. As they left, something made the back of The Kid's neck prickle. He wasn't a lawman, but he had some instincts of his own. He glanced back and saw the older stranger watching them intently. The man looked away, but not fast enough that The Kid missed his scrutiny.

He couldn't help wondering what that was about, and he was still curious when he saw the two men ride out of Chalk Butte a short time later.

Chapter 25

One thing Herb Tuttle had learned over the years was to never turn his back on a stroke of luck. So he was excited as he and Rowden rode toward the chalky-looking butte that gave the settlement its name. "Brick's gonna be mighty happy when he hears what we found out. We come all this way and the man he's lookin' for falls right into our laps."

"I don't give a damn about that," Rowden said with a surly frown on his face. "I want that blasted marshal who buffaloed me. My head hurts like hell, and he's got to pay for that." Rowden's eyes narrowed. "I wouldn't mind teachin' that deputy of his a lesson, too."

"That'll be up to Brick. But I've got a hunch as long as he gets his revenge on Tate, he won't care much what happens to the rest of the people in that town."

"You think there are enough of us to take it over?"

"You saw the place," Tuttle answered with a shrug. "If we take the citizens by surprise, they won't have a chance to fight back. If it was me, I'd hit 'em in the middle of the night, but that'll be up to Brick, too. He makes the plans."

"Better be a good one," Rowden growled. "As far as I'm concerned it's past time ridin' with this gang starts to pay off, and some of the other fellas feel the same way."

Tuttle knew Rowden was telling the truth. Discontent had spread throughout the gang, especially among the younger members. But if Cantrell's desire for revenge led to the looting of an entire town, the other outlaws would forget about their complaints quickly enough.

They rounded the butte with their heavily loaded horses. Tuttle spotted the rest of the men taking their ease while their horses grazed on the grass growing in the lee of the butte. Cantrell walked out a short distance to meet them, raising a hand in greeting.

"I see you got the supplies." He nodded toward the heavy packs lashed to their saddles.

"We got more than that." Tuttle swung down from the saddle and went on. "Guess who's in that town right now, Brick."

Cantrell frowned and snapped, "If you've got something to say, just spit it out, Herb. You know I'm not much for playing games."

"Sorry. It's Tate. Jared Tate. He and that fella Morgan are in Chalk Butte. From what I could gather, they're friends with the marshal there."

Cantrell's bushy, graying eyebrows rose in surprise. "Tate," he whispered. "This close."

Tuttle nodded. "Yeah, no doubt about it. I saw him myself and heard him called by name. Morgan, too."

"Son of a—" Cantrell stopped short and pounded his right fist into his left palm. "I never expected to find them so easy!"

Rowden said, "I'm not sure how easy it was. I got a gun barrel bent over my head by that damn marshal."

"You mean Tate?" Cantrell asked.

"No, the other one. The one who's actually the marshal in Chalk Butte."

Cantrell waved that off. "I don't give a damn about him. You can kill him if you want, Rowden. Makes no never mind to me."

A vicious grin creased Rowden's face. "I was hopin' you'd say that, boss."

"How does the town look?" Cantrell asked Tuttle.

"Ripe for the pickin'. If we hit the place hard and fast enough, we'll be in charge before the people who live there even know what's goin' on."

"Then they won't have any choice but to turn Tate over to us," Cantrell mused. "I can deal with him while the rest of you clean out all the businesses."

"That sounds like a good plan to me," Tuttle agreed with a nod. "When do you want to hit them?"

Cantrell glanced narrow-eyed at the sky. "It's pretty late in the day. We'll wait here until after it's dark . . . let the town settle down a little and then strike while most folks have already gone to sleep."

"That's just what I was thinking," Tuttle said. "Maybe round up some hostages as soon as we get there. Chances are they won't even put up a fight."

"Tate will," Cantrell declared. "So will Morgan, I expect, and the local star packer, too."

Rowden said, "The marshal's got a hellcat of a daughter who works as his deputy. Wouldn't surprise me if she puts up a better fight than most of the men in the town."

"Still, that's just four of them against all of us." Cantrell shook his head. "They won't have a chance, and finally, I'll settle up with Tate for the past ten years!"

The Kid and Tate ate dinner at Marshal Porter's house again that evening. When they went out on the porch after the meal, The Kid mentioned the odd look the older stranger had given them in the general store. "He acted like he didn't want me noticing, but I saw him watching us."

Porter was packing tobacco into his pipe for an after-dinner smoke. "He was probably just mad because his friend got knocked out. He should've been grateful it wasn't worse than that. I could've locked up the two of them for disturbing the peace."

"Maybe that was it," The Kid said, but he wasn't convinced. There had been something else provoking the man's interest in them.

He cast his mind back to that afternoon and tried to remember everything that was said inside the general store. Porter had called Marshal Tate by name, The Kid recalled, and that led him to speculate.

Tate had made quite a few enemies while he was packing a badge. The Kid had already seen ample proof of that. Maybe the stranger was another one of those. Given Tate's current mental state, there was a better than even chance he wouldn't recognize someone who was holding a grudge against him.

In that case, there was also a chance the man would double back to Chalk Butte and try to bushwhack the old lawman. It would be easy enough to do in the hotel.

"Marshal, I was thinking," The Kid said to Porter. "You've got a cot in your office, don't you?"

"Sure. Sometimes I have to spend the night there when I have a prisoner who has to be watched."

"How would it be if Marshal Tate and I spend the night there tonight?"

Porter frowned as he puffed on his pipe. He blew out a cloud of smoke and asked, "Why would you want to do that?"

"I was thinking that fella this afternoon might be somebody with a score to settle with Marshal Tate."

"Nonsense," Tate said. "I never saw that man before in my life, or the one with him, either."

"Maybe you just don't remember them, Marshal." The Kid tried not to sound too harsh about it.

"Of course I'd remember somebody who wanted to kill me," Tate insisted.

Porter glanced over at The Kid, no doubt recalling their conversation on the porch the previous night. "You're thinking the marshal's office would be safer than the hotel."

The Kid nodded. "It's got nice thick stone

walls, and nobody would think to look for us there."

"Not a bad idea. Probably not necessary, but still not a bad idea."

Tate shook his head. "I don't understand any of this."

"That's all right, Marshal," Porter said. "Actually, you'd be doing me a favor if you spent the night at the office. I don't like leaving it unattended. Somebody needs to be there in case anybody has some trouble to report."

"So . . . we'd be like unofficial deputies."

"You could say that," Porter agreed.

The Kid thought it was a good tactic to try.

"I don't mind the sound of that," Tate said. "You and your daughter have been so kind to us while we're here, and this would be a way to pay you back a little."

"Sure," Porter said. "It works out best for everybody that way."

"All right, fine. We'll be glad to help out, won't we, Kid?"

"Of course." The Kid gave Porter a grateful nod. "Maybe the marshal could stay here while I go back to the hotel and get some of our things?"

"Sounds good to me."

"What sounds good?" Holly asked as she came out onto the porch after finishing with the after-dinner chores.

"Marshal Tate and Mr. Morgan are going to spend the night at the office instead of the hotel," Porter said, giving her a meaningful look. "You know I don't like to leave the place empty."

"That's right," Holly said.

The Kid thought she looked like she didn't fully understand, but was willing to play along.

He picked up his hat from the porch beside the rocking chair where he'd been sitting. He stood up and put it on, saying, "I'll be back in a little while, as soon as I move a few things down there."

"Take your time," Porter said between puffs on his pipe. "It's a beautiful evening. The three of us will sit here and enjoy it, won't we, Marshal?"

"That we will," said Tate.

"Maybe I'd better come with you, Mr. Morgan," Holly suggested. "After all, the office is locked up, and you'll need somebody to let you in."

"I could give you the key—" Porter began, but he stopped when his daughter shot a sharp glance in his direction. After a second he continued. "Yeah, I guess it'd be better if an official deputy went along."

"Anyway, I don't particularly want to sit around listening to you two old war horses swapping stories," she said.

"Fine. Go along, both of you," Porter said with a grin.

As they walked along the street toward the

hotel, Holly said, "I hope you don't mind me volunteering to accompany you like that, Mr. Morgan."

"Call me Kid," he suggested, "and a man would have to be a fool to object to spending time with you, Miss Porter. Or would you rather I call you Deputy Porter?"

"I'd rather you call me Holly, Kid."

He chuckled. "I think I can do that."

He didn't have any interest in starting a romance with Holly Porter. For one thing, he had shied clear of such things for the most part since his wife's death, and for another, he and Tate would be moving on in another day or two, continuing their journey to Wichita. There wasn't time for anything serious to develop, and The Kid wasn't the sort of man to trifle with a woman's affections. Conrad Browning might have been, but those days were long past.

However, he didn't see anything wrong with enjoying Holly's company. She was certainly a pleasant companion.

When they reached the hotel, The Kid went up to the rooms he'd rented for himself and Tate. Since the rooms were already paid for, he didn't gather up all their gear, just what they would need for the night. When he went downstairs, Holly was waiting for him in the lobby.

"Why don't you tell me the truth, Kid?" she said as they walked toward the marshal's office.

"You're doing this because you think there might be some trouble."

"Marshal Tate made a lot of enemies in his time. We ran into some of them back up the trail. I didn't like the way one of those strangers was eyeing us this afternoon."

"You think he's got a score to settle with the marshal?"

"Could be."

"And that hotel's a cracker box," Holly mused. "Anybody could get in there without much trouble and start shooting."

"That's the general idea."

"Yeah, you'll be safer in the jail. And nobody would think to look for you there."

They reached the squat building that housed the marshal's office and jail. Holly unlocked the front door and led the way inside. She scraped a match to life and lit the lamp on the desk.

"There's a cot in the back room, and the sofa out here," she said. "It's not too uncomfortable if you watch out for the broken spring."

The Kid smiled, "I'll remember that." He dropped the gear on the sofa.

As he did so, she moved closer to him, and something stirred inside him. He had a feeling she wasn't looking for anything serious any more than he was, but he also had the distinct impression she was thinking about kissing him.

Fair enough, he supposed. As he looked at her,

sultry and beautiful in the soft lamplight, the thought of kissing her certainly crossed his mind . . .

And then abruptly disappeared as gunshots from somewhere in Chalk Butte suddenly ripped through the night.

Chapter 26

Holly turned and plunged toward the door. The Kid's hand shot out and gripped her arm, stopping her.

"Let me go!" she cried. "There's trouble out there!"

"And if you jerk that door open with the light still burning in here, you'll be a perfect target."

She muttered something under her breath, then said, "You're right." She turned back to the desk, leaned over, and blew out the lamp. Darkness engulfed the office.

The first flurry of shots had stopped, but then several more blasted, more sporadically paced.

Holly drew her gun as she pulled the door open and stepped out into the night. The Kid was right behind her, also with his Colt in his hand.

Muzzle flame stabbed redly from the darkness of an alley mouth diagonally across the street. Bullets whipped past The Kid and Holly and pinged against the stone wall behind them.

There was no cover out there, so The Kid looped his free arm around Holly's waist and hurled them backward through the door. He snapped a couple of shots at the alley as they fell through the opening. More bullets whined through the air above them.

The Kid rolled to the side and kicked the door closed. Bullets smacked into it but didn't penetrate the thick wood.

"Let . . . *go* . . . of me!" Holly panted. "What are you doing?"

"Saving your life," The Kid said as he let go of her.

He surged to his feet and went to one of the windows just as a bullet shattered it, spraying glass across the room. He recalled the windows were equipped with heavy shutters on the inside, and slammed them shut. Holly put her anger aside long enough to do the same at the other window.

"Is there a back door?" The Kid asked.

"Yes. I'll bar it."

"Good idea."

She was much more familiar with the office than he was, of course, and didn't need light to find her way around. He heard her cross the room and a moment later a *thunk!* sounded as the bar dropped in place to fasten the rear door.

The Kid pulled one of the shutters back slightly to make a narrow gap through which he could look. The bushwhackers across the street had stopped shooting. He figured they were in that alley to open fire on anyone who left the marshal's office.

"It sounds like the whole town's under attack," Holly said as she opened a shutter on the other window a crack. "Who would do such a thing?"

"I've got a hunch it has to do with that hombre who was giving us the skunk eye in the general store this afternoon."

"Some old enemy of Marshal Tate's? He must have brought a blasted army with him, from the sound of it!"

That comment stirred something in The Kid's memory. He didn't know if what he was thinking was possible or not, but he realized he couldn't rule it out.

"What's your father going to do when he hears all that shooting?"

"What do you think he's going to do?" Holly snapped. "He'll come to see what it's all about. He'll do whatever he can to protect the citizens."

The Kid knew she was right. Porter wouldn't want to put Jared Tate in harm's way, but his duty to the people of Chalk Butte would come first. Porter might tell Tate to stay put at the house, but it was also possible he would take the old lawman with him while he investigated the shooting.

In a fight like this, having Tate around might even come in handy. Danger seemed to bring out the best in him and prod his brain into working more like it once had.

"Will he try to make it here to the jail?" The Kid asked.

"He might. He knows that's where we were headed, and he'll want to know that I'm safe."

"This place is pretty sturdy. Meant to be easy to defend."

"We can't just sit tight!" Holly said. "Papa's out there somewhere. I need to go help him."

"Why don't you hole up here, and I'll slip out the back and see if I can find out what's going on? You can close and bar the door again behind me as soon as I'm out."

"I know my way around this town a lot better than you do, blast it! I'm the one who ought to be going out there."

"Yeah, but I've had more experience fighting killers," The Kid said bluntly.

"How do you know that?"

The Kid thought about all the pitched battles he had taken part in over the past few years. "Take my word for it. Somebody's got to hold down the fort here, in case your father and Marshal Tate show up, and you're the best one for the job."

"All right, go on," she snapped. "But if you get yourself shot to pieces, don't expect me to weep over your bloody corpse!"

"You wouldn't even shed a single tear?" The Kid asked, smiling in the darkness.

"Go on before I change my mind, damn it."

They closed and fastened the shutters again, then retreated to the back room where the rear door was located. For all The Kid knew, he'd be stepping into another ambush, but he had to risk it. They needed to know what the situation was so they could plan a counterattack.

Working by feel, he drew the bar from its brackets and set it aside.

"Bar the door again as soon as I'm out," he whispered to Holly. "And don't open it unless you're absolutely sure who's on the other side."

"I'm not a complete fool, you know. I've been a deputy for several years. I've handled my share of trouble."

Not any like this, The Kid thought. "All right. I'll see you later."

"Be careful, Kid."

"I intend to."

If it hadn't been pitch-dark in the hallway, he might have bent over and planted a quick kiss on her forehead. As it was, he'd probably miss, and that would be awkward.

He opened the door slightly and slid into the alley behind the jail with his Colt gripped tightly in his hand.

No shots rang out as the door closed behind him. He heard the bar drop back in its brackets and felt a little better. Holly wasn't safe, by any means—he had a hunch nobody in Chalk Butte was truly safe at that moment—but she had a better chance with those stone walls and thick doors between her and the raiders, whoever they were.

The Kid moved along the rear wall of the jail until he reached the corner. Instinct made him pause there, and a second later, when he heard the faint scrape of boot leather against the ground, he understood why. Even though he hadn't been consciously aware of it, he had known someone was skulking around in the thick shadows next to the building.

He pressed himself against the wall and waited, breathing so shallowly it couldn't be heard more than an inch or two away. A few feet away, a deeper patch of darkness shifted. The Kid's keen eyes gradually made out the shapes of two men working stealthily toward him.

They stopped, and for a second he thought they might have spotted him, but then he heard a whisper.

"There's nobody back here."

"Doesn't matter," the second man whispered in return. "The boss said to watch the door and if anybody tries to sneak out, ventilate 'em."

"What if it's the hombre he's after? He'll be mighty upset if somebody else kills him."

"Yeah, but the main thing is, he don't want the old coot to get away, no matter who winds up killin' him."

The Kid's hunch was right. The men were after Marshal Jared Tate. The old lawman must have been one hell of a fine lawman to make so many enemies among the outlaw breed, The Kid thought.

"I'll take one side of the door, you take the other," one of the men suggested. "If anybody comes out, we'll have him in a crossfire."

"Just be careful we don't shoot each other."

That drew a grim chuckle from the first man as he stepped past The Kid, no more than two feet away.

The outlaw had no idea how close he was to death.

The Kid remained motionless until the two men were in position flanking the jail's rear door. Then he made his move, coming up behind the closest one, looping an arm around the man's neck, and jerking back to stifle any outcry as he pressed the barrel of his Colt into the man's side.

"Ssst!" the other outlaw hissed. "Davey, you say something?"

The Kid pressed down hard, cutting off the man's air. The man didn't dare struggle with that gun in his side, and after a moment he slumped in The Kid's grip as he passed out.

The Kid let go of him, allowing him to fall to the ground with a soft *thud*. Hearing it, the other outlaw leaped forward, raising his voice a little as he whispered urgently, "Davey!"

The Kid pressed the muzzle of his Colt against the outlaw's forehead. "Davey can't hear you."

With a startled gasp, the man jerked back involuntarily, raising his gun slightly.

The Kid leaped forward and slashed with his revolver, feeling the barrel strike yielding flesh. He chopped down again, and the gun landed with the solid thud of metal against bone. The outlaw fell to his knees and pitched forward.

The Kid reversed his Colt and used the butt to rap on the back door of the jail. He gave Holly a moment to get there. She didn't say anything, and he gave her credit for being cautious. Hoping she was there to hear him, he said, "Holly, it's me, Kid Morgan. Open up. I've got a couple prisoners."

"Kid?" The whisper came through the tiny crack around the door. "How do I know they don't have a gun on you?"

"Because I'd let them shoot me before I'd betray you," he answered honestly.

That satisfied her. The bar scraped in its brackets, and then the door swung inward. Holly stepped, into the doorway, gun in hand.

"Cover me," The Kid told her as he bent to grasp the collar of one of the unconscious outlaws. He dragged the man inside and, working by feel, put him in a cell. It took him only a moment to haul the other man inside, then Holly closed and barred the door.

The Kid dumped the second man inside the same cell and made sure neither of the prisoners had any more guns or knives, then slammed the cell door. "Bring the lamp," he told Holly.

She came back with it and lit it.

The yellow glow revealed the hard, beard-stubbled faces of the two raiders. One of them had an ugly gash on his face where The Kid's gun sight had raked him. Both men were beginning to stir.

"Whoever the boss of this gang is, he sent these two to watch the back door," The Kid explained. "They didn't get here quite soon enough. I was able to jump them."

"That's pretty good work, taking them both without firing a shot," Holly said as she glanced at The Kid with a new level of respect.

He didn't care about that. "Hold the light closer." He drew his Colt again and pointed it at the two men. "Wake up, fellas, unless you'd rather die without seeing it coming."

The man The Kid had choked to unconsciousness groaned and rolled over. He lifted his head and shook it groggily, then raised it even more so he could look up at his captors.

The Kid had never seen the man before, but was still convinced the attack on the town had something to do with the two men who'd been in the general store that afternoon. He eared back the hammer of his gun and aimed it at the man's face. "You'd better talk, or I won't have any reason to keep you alive. Who's behind this? What does he want?"

"Who . . . who are you, mister?" the outlaw mumbled.

"Never mind that. Just answer the questions."

"You'll find out soon enough." The man sneered. "Our boss will wipe out the whole town if he has to, to get what he wants."

"And that's Marshal Jared Tate, isn't it?"

"Go to hell," the man snapped. "I'm not talkin'."

"Well, then . . ." The Kid's finger tightened on the trigger.

He wasn't really going to blow the man's brains out, but obviously his bluff was convincing. Holly exclaimed, "Kid, wait! You can't—"

"Don't shoot!" the outlaw said, his eyes wide with fear. "I don't reckon it matters whether you know or not. There's nothing you can do about it. The boss has got fifty townspeople rounded up and herded into the church, and he'll kill all of them if he don't get what he wants."

"And that is?" The Kid thought he already knew the answer, but the next moment his hunch was confirmed. Not by the prisoner inside the cell, however, but by a powerful shout from the street outside.

"Tate! Marshal Jared Tate! I know you hear me! This is Brick Cantrell, and if you don't come out and face me, the blood of this whole town will be on your head!"

Chapter 27

He had suspected he knew who was behind the attack on Chalk Butte, but hearing Brick Cantrell's voice still came as a shock to The Kid.

Not that he had ever heard Cantrell's voice before, of course. The shock came more from having been told Cantrell was still in prison and believing that to be true. Whether he had escaped from custody or been released, in the end it didn't matter.

The only important thing was that Cantrell had hostages under the guns of him and his men, and was demanding vengeance on Marshal Jared Tate.

The man inside the cell laughed. "Not so damned smart now, are you?"

For a second The Kid thought about shooting him—just a nice flesh wound in the leg, maybe—but pushed that idea aside. He wasn't going to descend to the same level as these vicious outlaws.

"What are we going to do?" Holly asked tensely.

"Come on." The Kid led the way back out into the marshal's office and closed the cell block door, plunging the cells back into darkness. When Holly set the lamp on the desk, he told her, "Blow that out again."

Once more shadows cloaked the office as Holly

blew out the flame. Out in the street Cantrell shouted, "Tate! Did you hear me, old man? I'll kill all those people! Men, women, and children, Tate!"

"He's crazy," Holly whispered. "Pure loco."

"He's had ten years in prison to get that way, if he wasn't to start with," The Kid said. "Where's that church he mentioned?"

"There are three in town. I don't know which one he's talking about. Do you think we can get to the hostages and free them?"

"That's what I had in mind. He thinks the back door here is covered. He doesn't know we took care of the men he sent back there."

"So we can get out, and they won't know we're on the loose."

"Right. But the two of us can't do much good against all of them unless we have some sort of plan."

"We need to find my father and Marshal Tate," Holly said. "Or will the marshal surrender himself to Cantrell?"

"I don't think your father would let him do that, even if he wanted to."

"Neither do I," Holly agreed. "We need to get out there. We can work our way back toward the house, and maybe we'll meet Papa and Marshal Tate on the way."

The Kid thought about it for a second and then nodded, even though his companion couldn't see him in the dark. "They'll head for the jail, we'll head for them. Sounds like it might work. But there's something we need to do first. We can't leave those prisoners able to yell and warn Cantrell."

"What are you going to do?" Holly asked. "We can't just kill them in cold blood."

"Maybe not, but we can make sure they stay quiet."

They took the lamp into the cell block and lit it again. Both outlaws were conscious. The one with the blood-smeared face glared murderously at The Kid.

"Tie him up and gag him," The Kid told the other man.

"What if I tell you to go to hell instead?" the outlaw responded with a sneer.

"Then I just shoot you both and be done with it."

"You're bluffing."

The Kid shrugged. "Maybe you're right. It would be quieter and attract less attention if I just cut your throats. Mighty efficient, too."

"Better do what he says," Bloody Face advised. "I think he's crazy enough to do it."

His partner gave in. He tore strips off his shirt and used them to bind Bloody Face's wrists behind his back, then fashioned a gag with more scraps of cloth.

Once that was done, The Kid said, "All right, come up here by the bars and turn around."

"You're gonna knock me out, aren't you?" the man asked with a sigh.

"There's still the throat-cutting option," The Kid reminded him.

The outlaw did as he was told. The Kid's gun rose and fell, striking through the bars. The outlaw crumpled to the floor, out cold.

Holly unlocked the door then. The Kid dragged the unconscious man into another cell and tied and gagged him. Separated like that, the two outlaws couldn't try to free each other. Satisfied they had done all they could, Holly relocked the cell doors and she and The Kid left the cell block.

At the back door, she blew out the lamp again.

"I'll go first," The Kid said as he unbarred the rear door.

"You know, you started giving orders mighty easy there," Holly said. "I'm the peace officer here, not you."

"Didn't mean to step on your toes. I was just doing what made sense."

"Oh, go ahead. If I don't agree with something, I'll let you know."

The Kid didn't doubt that for a second.

With guns drawn, they slipped into the alley and paused to listen intently. Out in the street, Cantrell shouted, "Tate! Where are you? I'm going to start shooting the townspeople, one by one, unless you show yourself!"

"He won't get away with this." it was a promise The Kid intended to keep.

There hadn't been any shooting since Cantrell started trying to draw out Marshal Tate, but gunfire erupted again, somewhere a block or two away.

"Someone's in trouble!" Holly said. "We have to go help them!" She hurried toward the sound of the shots.

The Kid caught up to her in a couple quick strides. "That could be a trick to lure us into the open."

"Can't take that chance," Holly snapped. "People's lives could be in danger."

The Kid knew she was right about that. He trotted alongside her as they moved quickly through the night shadows.

They paused at the rear corner of a building. The Kid leaned over to take a look toward Main Street. Someone appeared to be pinned down behind some barrels at the mouth of the narrow passage between buildings. Bullets whined and sizzled around him and threw splinters from the barrels into the air and the walls of the buildings.

Whoever was behind the barrels returned the fire briefly before being forced to duck down again. Those muzzle flashes lit up the gunman's face enough for The Kid to recognize Marshal Bob Porter. He saw a second person in the brief flashes and felt sure it was Tate crouched with

Porter, although the Chalk Butte lawman was the only one shooting.

Holly recognized her father, too, and called, "Papa! Back here!"

Porter jerked around in surprise, then grabbed Tate by the arm and dragged him along as he ran through the passage toward his daughter and The Kid. "Holly!" he cried. "Is that you? Are you all right?"

"I'm fine," she told him as they threw their arms around each other. "But we've got to stop those men and free the hostages!"

"I know. I was hoping we'd find you—"

The reunion was rudely interrupted by gunshots ripping apart the darkness from the far corner of the building. The raiders had sent several men circling around to catch Porter and Tate from behind.

Those gunmen got more than they bargained for. The Kid was already whirling around to meet this new threat even as the shots began to blast. His Colt roared and bucked in his hand as he aimed at the muzzle flashes. Porter and Holly were only a hair slower in their reactions as they joined in the fight. Keeping Tate behind them, they pulled back into the dubious shelter of the narrow opening between buildings.

"We can't stay here," Porter said between shots. "They'll charge us from the other direction and catch us in a crossfire."

"Then let's do what they won't expect and meet them head-on," The Kid suggested as he thumbed fresh rounds into his Colt. "I'll lead the way."

"Right behind you," Porter said. "Holly, keep an eye on Marshal Tate."

The Kid didn't wait to hear if Holly was going to object to being given that responsibility. He charged into the alley behind the buildings, the gun in his hand roaring and spitting flame and lead.

Thinking their quarry was trapped in the gap between buildings, the would-be killers hadn't bothered to take cover. The sudden counterattack took them by surprise, and as muzzle flashes cast their hellish glare over the alley and lit it up almost as bright as day, The Kid saw men spinning off their feet as slugs ripped into them. He felt the tug of a bullet on his coat and hoped those behind him were safe.

The raiders who were still on their feet broke and ran in the face of the fierce assault. The Kid and Porter sent them on their way with a few last shots.

"Holly," Porter said urgently as he lowered his gun. "Are you hit?"

"No, Papa, I'm fine," she replied. "So is Marshal Tate."

"Cantrell's here. Brick Cantrell. I have to arrest him," Tate exclaimed.

"I hope you get the chance to do just that, Marshal," The Kid said. "Right now we've got to find those hostages and see if we can free them. One of Cantrell's men said he had them locked up in a church. You have any idea which one, Marshal Porter?"

The local lawman shook his head and gave the same answer Holly had earlier. "Could be any of the three—"

A bell began to toll in the night. It went on for a long moment, then as the sound began to die off in echoes, Cantrell shouted, "You hear that, Tate? That's a funeral bell for those hostages if you don't face me like a man right now!"

"I know that bell," Holly said breathlessly. "It's the one in the Baptist Church."

"Then that's probably where they are," The Kid said. "We don't have anything else to go on. Can you get us there without running into any more of Cantrell's men?"

"Can't guarantee that," Porter said, "but we can get there, that's for sure. Come on."

"I . . . I should go face him, like he wants," Tate said.

The Kid took the old lawman's arm. "Not now, Marshal. Maybe later, if it comes to that, but not now. We need you with us."

"All right," Tate said, but he didn't sound convinced. "I'll come with you."

"Lead the way, Holly," Porter said. "I'll bring up the rear."

It was a good thing Holly knew where she was

going, The Kid thought as he followed the twisting, turning route she took through Chalk Butte's alleys and back streets. They were all alert, knowing they might run into more of Cantrell's men at any moment.

They paused as Cantrell bellowed, "I warned you, Tate! I warned you!"

The shout was followed by a single gunshot.

"Oh!" Holly exclaimed in horror. "Did . . . did he just—"

"We'll have to worry about that later," The Kid said in a flat, grim tone. "The sooner we free the hostages, the fewer people will lose their lives."

"Mr. Morgan's right, Holly," Porter said. "Let's go."

They resumed their trek through the shadows, and a few moments later, Holly came to a stop at the mouth of an alley across the street from a large church with a bell tower and steeple. Lights burned brightly inside it, and men holding rifles were ranged around it.

"No doubt about it," Porter said quietly. "That's where they've got the hostages. But how in blazes are we going to get in there?"

"Cantrell probably has men inside, too, with orders to start shooting the prisoners if the place comes under attack," The Kid said. "We have to force them out of there some way."

Tate said, "What about . . . what about if we set the church on fire?"

251

The others turned to look at him. After a moment Marshal Porter said, "There are fifty prisoners in there."

"I know outlaws," Tate said, his voice growing stronger. "They don't care about anybody but themselves. They'll forget all about the prisoners if it means saving their own hides."

"The marshal might be right about that," The Kid said. "If we can get somebody into the church to lead the prisoners out, they'd stand a chance of surviving, anyway." He looked at Porter. "It's your decision, Marshal."

Porter frowned, deep in thought for several seconds, but then he sighed and nodded. "We'll have to give it a try. We can get a jug of kerosene from the general store, make a fuse of some sort, and heave it up on the church roof."

Tate said, "I could still go out there and meet Cantrell face-to-face. That's what he wants."

"That may be what he wants," The Kid said, "but the rest of his men won't be satisfied with that. I'll bet they're planning on looting the whole town, and there's no telling how many people will be killed if they do."

"I agree with Mr. Morgan," Porter said. "Nobody doubts your courage, Marshal Tate, but if you surrender you'll be throwing your life away for nothing."

"All right, then," Tate agreed. "Let's see about getting those people out of there."

Chapter 28

The first order of business was to get their hands on some kerosene. Porter said, "You three stay here. I'll go back to the general store. I can break in and get a jug of kerosene without much trouble, I think."

"One of us should go with you," Holly protested. "If you run into any of Cantrell's men, you'll need help."

Porter shook his head. "No, if anything happens to me, I want the three of you to be able to carry on without me. We don't want to split our forces in half."

"That makes sense," The Kid agreed. "Good luck, Marshal."

Porter cat-footed off into the darkness with Holly anxiously watching him go.

The minutes ticked by with maddening slowness as they waited for Porter to return. To help pass the time and distract her from worrying about her father, The Kid asked Holly about the layout of the church.

"There's a small door in the back that leads through a storeroom and then into the sanctuary."

"That's the way we'll need to get in."

"They're sure to have it guarded."

"We'll deal with that when the time comes,"

The Kid said. "Once we're inside, your father and I will take care of any outlaws that are left while you get the townspeople out."

"Why do you give me that job?" she demanded. "I can shoot, too, you know."

"I know, but there'll be women and children among those hostages, and I figure they'll be more likely to follow you. In the middle of a bunch of fear and confusion, to them your father and I will just be two more men with guns."

Holly pondered that for a moment before nodding. "What you say makes sense," she admitted reluctantly. "But if I need to get right in the middle of the fight, I will."

"I wouldn't expect anything else from you," The Kid told her honestly.

A few minutes later, the soft pad of rapidly approaching footsteps made them turn quickly with guns drawn. Marshal Bob Porter came out of the shadows, carrying something that sloshed as he trotted up to them.

He lifted the jug of kerosene. "Got it. I'll settle up with the storekeeper later for the jug and for the damage I did to his back door."

"If we can save the town from being looted, I think he'll be glad to call it square," Holly said. "I was worried about you, Papa."

"No need to worry." Porter's teeth flashed in a grin. "Let's get this done. We'll have to circle around to come at the church from the back."

"Hold on a minute," The Kid snapped. "Who's this?"

From the concealing darkness of the alley, they watched as several men strode toward the church, led by a tall man with graying red hair.

"That must be Cantrell," Porter whispered. "I remembered after all this started that I'd heard he was released from prison. I knew I'd heard something about him, but I couldn't think of what it was until then. Maybe if I had . . ."

"It wouldn't have made any difference," The Kid said. "Nobody would have expected him to waltz in here and take over the whole town like this."

"Not the whole town," Holly reminded him. "We're still loose. We can still make a difference."

Across the street, Brick Cantrell came to a stop and told his men in a loud, compelling voice, "Bring out another hostage. A woman this time."

In the alley, Holly breathed, "Oh, no," and her father muttered a curse. The Kid just looked on, his mouth a taut, grim line across his face.

"We can't just stand by and let him murder someone else," Porter said.

"We won't," Tate said, and that made The Kid look around quickly. He made a grab for the old lawman, but Tate moved with surprising speed, lunging past Porter and Holly and running out into the street.

"Cantrell!" Tate shouted. "Cantrell, this ends now!"

It was about to end catastrophically, The Kid sensed, but maybe they could save the people in the church, anyway. He grabbed the jug of kerosene from Porter. "Split up! Come at them from three directions! Holly, get in that church and get those people out!"

He raced out into the street as Cantrell swung around and bellowed, "Tate! At last!"

The Kid heaved the jug as hard as he could and dove forward, tackling Tate from behind and knocking him to the ground as Cantrell opened fire. Bullets screamed through the air just above them.

Lifting his Colt, The Kid tracked the jug as it flew through the air. The revolver blasted, and the jug came apart as the bullet struck, spraying kerosene all over Cantrell and the dozen or so outlaws standing near him in front of the church.

One man fired his gun without thinking, and that was all it took. The kerosene on his hand ignited, and flames engulfed his fingers and raced up the sleeve of his shirt as he screamed. The nightmarish sight was all it took to make the other outlaws hesitate about pulling their triggers.

Porter and Holly quickly burst out of the alley and split up, Porter going left while Holly went right. They fired on the run, cutting down several outlaws.

Cantrell let out an incoherent howl of rage and cast his gun aside, then charged toward The Kid and Tate.

The Kid could have shot him, but Tate tore loose from him and scrambled up, getting in the line of fire. The Kid swung his Colt toward the remaining outlaws instead and triggered three times, putting two more men on the ground.

The man who had set his arm on fire had fallen to the ground, igniting more of the kerosene. Flames raced here and there in the street. The men who had gotten the volatile stuff all over them were more concerned with staying away from the fire than they were with putting up a fight, which made them easy targets for The Kid, Porter, and Holly.

The thunder of hoofbeats made The Kid roll over and come up on one knee. He reloaded quickly as he saw more of the gang racing along Main Street. They hadn't been doused with kerosene, so they blazed away at the three people making a gallant stand for Chalk Butte.

The Kid snapped his gun closed and brought it up to blow one of the charging outlaws out of the saddle. Then he flung himself to the side to avoid being trampled as the horses pounded past him. He rolled over and fired from his belly, his shot rewarded by the sight of a badman throwing his hands in the air and pitching limply off his horse.

From where he lay The Kid suddenly caught sight of Jared Tate and Brick Cantrell, locked in a fierce hand-to-hand struggle in the middle of the street. Cantrell was younger, bigger, and stronger, and Tate shouldn't have been any match for him.

Somewhere inside him, though, Tate had found reserves of strength, and the blows he sledged into Cantrell's face and body rocked the outlaw with unexpected power. Tate bored in, driving Cantrell back a few steps.

Cantrell caught himself and recovered from the surprise of the fierce battle Tate was putting up. He blocked one of Tate's punches and batted the old lawman's arm aside. Cantrell's fist shot in and smashed Tate in the face. Tate lost his footing and flew backward. Cantrell leaped after him. Landing on top of Tate, he closed his hands around his old enemy's throat, clearly intent on choking the life out of him.

The Kid surged to his feet and drew a bead on Cantrell. The range was a little long, but he thought he could put a bullet through the boss outlaw's head.

Before he could squeeze the trigger, a charging horse's shoulder clipped him from behind, knocking him down again. The Colt flew out of The Kid's hand.

He lay there for a second, stunned, before he was able to get up. As he came to his hands and knees and lurched to his feet, he knew there was no time to look for his gun. He broke into a run toward Cantrell and Tate.

When he was still a couple yards away, The Kid launched himself into the air. The diving tackle sent him crashing into Cantrell. The impact sent both men rolling through the dust of the street. The Kid came up first by a heartbeat and let fly with a haymaker that caught Cantrell squarely on the jaw and staggered him.

Cantrell recovered almost instantly and charged. The Kid was between him and Tate, and Cantrell's hate-distorted face made it plain that he was willing to go through anything to get to the man he wanted to kill.

The Kid was equally determined to stop him. He absorbed the punishment as Cantrell's rock-hard fists pounded into him and slugged right back at the outlaw chief. All around them, flames leaped and guns roared and people shouted and screamed, but for those two men nothing else in the world existed at that moment, only their anger and determination and the pain they could deal out to each other.

The reek of kerosene soaking Cantrell's clothes bit into The Kid's nose. He ignored it and kept fighting. The battle moved back and forth across the street, swaying first one way then the other as each man in turn was forced to give ground.

The Kid sensed he was slowly gaining the

advantage. Cantrell's arms seemed to be moving slower when he threw his punches. The outlaw's face was swollen and bleeding from the damage The Kid had inflicted. His chest heaved as he struggled to catch his breath.

Cantrell realized he was losing and reached behind his back, producing a knife. The Kid jerked backward to avoid the blade's sweeping thrust. A mere couple inches separated him from having his guts spilled out.

While The Kid was off balance, Cantrell stuck a foot out and hooked it between The Kid's ankles. The Kid went down, and Cantrell raised the knife high as he leaped forward, aiming to plunge the blade into The Kid's chest.

Somewhere nearby, a gun roared.

A shudder went through Cantrell's body as the bullet drove into his chest. The impact brought his attack to an abrupt halt, but didn't cause him to drop the knife. He stumbled forward a step, and the gun blasted again.

The Kid rolled to the side and came up on his knees. Jared Tate stood with a revolver gripped in both hands. Smoke curled from the muzzle. Flames lit up the old lawman's grim face as he fired again and again.

The slugs hammered into Brick Cantrell's body and made the outlaw do a grotesque dance. The knife slipped from his fingers and thudded to the ground.

Sheer willpower seemed to be all that was keeping Cantrell on his feet as blood welled from his wounds. Willpower, and pure hate. His face contorted in a snarl as he said, "Tate, you . . . you old . . . you . . ."

Whatever venom he wanted to spew, he couldn't finish. He collapsed, falling first to his knees and then pitching forward on his face, not to move again.

The Kid spotted his gun lying on the ground and hurried to scoop it up. As he did, he looked around and saw bodies scattered up and down the street. The doors of the church were wide open, and people stood in front of the building holding each other and crying or asking questions. The shooting seemed to be over.

Marshal Tate still stood with the gun thrust out in front of him. The Kid moved over to him, put his hand on the revolver, and gently pushed it down. "Looks like it's over, Marshal. You finished off Brick Cantrell."

"After all this time . . ." Tate murmured. He glanced at The Kid with the light of understanding in his eyes. It might not last, probably wouldn't last, but for now Tate knew what had just happened.

"Kid!"

The cry from Holly made The Kid swing around. He saw her running toward him, apparently unhurt. Her father limped along behind her with a bloodstain on his trouser leg, but didn't seem to be injured too badly.

For a second, The Kid thought Holly was going to throw her arms around him, but she stopped before she let herself get completely carried away. "Are you all right?"

The Kid took hold of his chin, worked his jaw back and forth, and grimaced. "I'll be sore and bruised in the morning from that pounding Cantrell gave me, but it's nothing to worry about." He turned to look at Porter. "Are the outlaws all dead, Marshal?"

"Dead or wounded bad enough they won't put up a fight anymore," Porter confirmed. "That is, the ones who didn't light a shuck out of here when they saw the fight going against them. When Holly shot down the guards in the church and freed the hostages, some of the townsmen got their hands on guns and started getting even with Cantrell's men. That tipped the balance in our favor."

The Kid nodded. When good men stood up to evil, things didn't always work out in their favor. But when good men did nothing, evil always won.

"So you shot it out with the guards in the church, did you?" he asked Holly with a smile.

"I told you I can handle a gun," she said with a characteristically defiant toss of her head.

"That you did," The Kid agreed. "I'm glad we were on the same side."

"We've got some prisoners to round up and put in jail," Porter said.

"I can give you a hand with that," Tate offered.

"Thanks, Marshal. I'll take you up on it."

The two lawmen moved off to handle mopping up after the battle. Several armed townsmen came out to help them.

"We were lucky," Holly said quietly to The Kid. "What Marshal Tate did could have gotten us all killed."

"He sure stood tall there at the end, though, didn't he?"

"He did," she agreed with a smile.

"Not everyone gets a last hurrah like that," The Kid said. "I think Jared Tate just made the most of his."

Chapter 29

Marshal Bob Porter's leg wound wasn't bad enough to keep him from getting around, but The Kid thought it might be a good idea to stay in Chalk Butte for a few more days, just in case any more trouble cropped up. Holly was an able deputy, but the law could always use a helping hand.

Also, after the punishment they had taken,

neither The Kid nor Jared Tate felt like getting in the saddle and riding for several more days to Wichita. Since there was no hurry, they stayed and rested up a little first.

Porter sent a wire to the county sheriff, advising him of the prisoners he was holding in his jail, the remnants of the gang Brick Cantrell had put together. All of them were wanted outlaws, so the sheriff was glad to travel to Chalk Butte with some deputies and take them off Porter's hands.

With that taken care of, the town settled back into being the peaceful little community it had been before The Kid and Tate rode in. Well, peaceful other than the occasional visit from the Boomhausers . . .

One evening The Kid and Porter sat on the front porch of the marshal's house. Tate had offered to dry the dishes for Holly, so the two of them were still inside.

Porter took his pipe out of his mouth and said, "I reckon you'll be leaving pretty soon."

"I set out to take Marshal Tate back to his daughter's place," The Kid said. "I suppose I need to get around to it, even though the past few days here have been mighty pleasant."

"Don't take this the wrong way," Porter said, "but I think it's best you move on, too. Holly's taken a real liking to you, Kid, but I've got a hunch you're not the sort of man to stay in one place for too long. That usually spells trouble for a woman who's grown fond of you."

"I'd never do anything to hurt your daughter, Marshal. You have my word on that."

"Not on purpose, maybe, but when you ride away it's gonna hurt her anyway. It'll just get worse the longer you're here."

The Kid chuckled. "That sounds like you're telling me to get out of town."

"Not exactly. But since you're going to be leaving anyway . . ."

"I understand," The Kid said.

"Now, Jared, on the other hand, I'll be sorry to see him go. He's a fine hombre, and he's been mighty helpful around here. I know he's got to get back home, though."

"Maybe his daughter will bring him back to visit sometime," The Kid suggested.

"Maybe." Porter didn't sound like he believed that would happen. "He's already forgotten the battle with Cantrell. He won't remember any of us for very long."

The Kid sighed. "I'm afraid you're right about that."

The next morning he got their gear together and saddled their horses. Holly, who was walking past the stable, saw him and exclaimed, "What are you doing?"

"Getting ready to ride," The Kid told her. "Marshal Tate and I still need to get to Wichita."

"You weren't going to tell me?" Holly asked with a frown. "You were just going to ride off without saying good-bye?"

"I didn't say that. Anyway, your father knows about this."

"He didn't say anything to me!" She was visibly upset.

The Kid had steered clear of spending any time alone with her, and he hadn't done anything that she could have mistaken for a romantic advance. But the feelings were there regardless, and The Kid understood. He felt drawn to her, too. If things had been different . . .

But they weren't, and he had long since learned that brooding too much about such things led only to madness.

"Do you think you'll ever ride this way again?" Holly asked.

"That's hard to say. I can't rule it out."

"But you can't promise it, either."

"I don't like to make promises if I don't know whether I can keep them," The Kid said. "I sort of go where the wind takes me these days."

She blew out her breath in exasperation. "Like some dime novel hero?"

He thought about Kid Morgan's origins for a second, then said, "More than you know."

Marshal Tate didn't seem to be too fond of the idea of leaving Chalk Butte, but he went along without causing any trouble. He shook hands

266

with Porter, and then Holly hugged him. "You're welcome back here any time, Marshal."

"Why, thank you, ma'am," Tate said with a smile. "What was your name again?"

"It's . . . Holly," she replied with a catch in her voice.

"Of course." Still smiling, Tate patted her on the shoulder. "Good-bye, Holly."

Porter shook hands with The Kid. "Good luck on the rest of your journey. If you think about it, send me a wire to let us know you got there all right."

"I'll do that," The Kid promised.

He turned toward his buckskin, but Holly was there. She put her arms around him, but it was no affectionate hug like the one she had given Tate. She twined her arms around his neck and pulled his head down so her mouth found his in a passionate kiss. When she broke away a moment later, she grinned. "There. I wanted you to know what you're riding away from."

"Believe me. I know."

It took a considerable amount of willpower for The Kid to swing up into the saddle and put Chalk Butte behind him.

When he looked back, Holly and her father were waving. The Kid and Marshal Tate lifted their arms in farewell and kept riding.

Wichita was a big town. Nothing like New York or Boston or San Francisco, of course, or even

St. Louis or Denver. But compared to places like Chalk Butte or Copperhead Springs, Wichita was a real metropolis.

Constance had given Bertha Edwards's address to The Kid back in Copperhead Springs. He asked directions and found the street without too much trouble. It was lined with cottonwoods. The shoes on their horses' hooves rang against the paving stones as The Kid and Marshal Tate rode along looking for the Edwards's house.

It was a nice neighborhood, the sort of place where normal families lived. At least, that's what The Kid thought. He couldn't be sure, he reminded himself, because he'd never been part of a normal family. Growing up, his mother had been one of the richest women in the country, and after her death he had found himself in the position of taking over the vast Browning business and financial empire.

Oh, and his real father had turned out to be one of the most notorious gunfighters in the Old West, a living legend who still roamed the frontier as one of the last of that dying breed. So, no, he thought wryly, not really a normal family anywhere in his background.

But his past had made him the man he was, and he could live with that.

"I think this is it," he told Marshal Tate as he drew rein in front of a small, neat house with whitewashed walls, flower boxes under the windows, and a picket fence around the yard. "Does the place look familiar to you, Marshal?"

"I don't think I've ever seen this house before," Tate replied with a nervous edge in his voice. "Who is it that's supposed to live here?"

"Your daughter Bertha and her husband Tim. Their last name is Edwards."

Tate sighed. "If you say so." Clearly he didn't have any idea who The Kid was talking about.

The Kid tightened his jaw and held in the sigh wanting to escape. He was filled with the fervent hope he would never fall victim to whatever malady had claimed Jared Tate. It was more than simple old age.

Given the dangerous life he led, the chances he would live long enough to worry about that were pretty slim, he thought.

They dismounted and tied their horses to the fence. The Kid opened the gate and ushered Tate through it onto the walk leading to a small porch. They went up the steps, and The Kid knocked on the door.

He immediately saw the resemblance between Marshal Tate and the woman who opened the door. She was lean, with faded blond hair, and looked somewhat older than her years.

The Kid took off his hat. "Mrs. Edwards?"

She ignored him, staring past him at Tate with slowly widening eyes. "Papa? Is that really you?"

"Hello," Tate said in a polite, neutral tone of voice, making it clear he didn't know her.

Bertha Edwards's mouth twisted briefly in a grimace. She looked at The Kid. "You're Mr. Morgan?"

"That's right, ma'am."

"I got a wire from Marshal Cumberland in Copperhead Springs saying you were bringing my father home." She opened the screen door. "Come on in, I suppose."

"Thank you," The Kid nodded. He touched Tate's arm and inclined his head toward the door. "Let's go, Marshal."

"All right." Tate was being cooperative, but that was all.

Bertha ushered them into a nicely furnished parlor. "Can I get you something, Mr. Morgan? Some coffee?"

"That would be fine, thank you," The Kid said.

"I could use some coffee, too," Tate said.

"Of course, Papa." She gestured toward armchairs. "Go ahead and sit down."

When Bertha had left the room and The Kid and Tate had taken their seats, the old lawman leaned over and said quietly, "She keeps calling me Papa."

"That's because she's your daughter, Marshal," The Kid explained patiently. "You need to try hard to remember her."

"Are you sure about that?" Tate asked with a

frown. "My daughter lives in Copperhead Springs with my wife. We're not in Copperhead Springs, are we?"

"No. Things have changed since the time you remember."

"I don't see how," Tate said with heartbreaking sincerity.

Bertha came back into the room with cups of coffee on a tray. She handed them to The Kid and Tate, then sat down on a sofa across from them with the tray on her knees.

"Thank you for bringing him home, Mr. Morgan. I can't tell you how worried I've been about him."

"Yes, ma'am, I'm sure."

"Did you have any trouble along the way? I expected you to be here sooner."

"There was . . . a little trouble," The Kid said. "Nothing to worry about, though. Your father is fine."

She let out a snort and shook her head. "He's not fine." Her voice was heavy with bitterness. "He'll never be fine. Not the way he is now."

"Well, I mean . . . he . . ." The Kid didn't know what to say. For one of the few times in his life he was speechless, and he didn't like the feeling.

Bertha shook her head again. "I'm sorry. I shouldn't let that out. It's just difficult."

"I'm sure it is."

"I can pay you for your time and trouble getting him here," she went on. "My husband doesn't make a great deal of money—he's a clerk in a law office—but we have a little set aside . . ."

"That's not necessary at all." The Kid took a sip of the coffee. Not surprising, it was bitter, too. "I was headed this direction anyway," He went on, stretching the truth, "and I was glad to have your father's company on the trail."

"Kid," Tate said, "when are we leaving? We need to get back to Copperhead Springs."

Bertha didn't give The Kid a chance to answer. She said sharply, "You're not going back to Copperhead Springs. You don't live there any-more. Mama's dead. You could remember that if you'd just try."

Tate blinked at the rebuke, obviously confused.

Bertha looked at The Kid. "Again, I'm sorry, Mr. Morgan. I'm glad to see him, I really am, and I'm grateful to you, but he . . . he's just so damned frustrating!"

"Yes, ma'am." The Kid's nerves were taut. He would have rather faced another horde of rampaging outlaws than deal with a situation like that. He set the cup on a small side table and stood up. "I should be going."

"Wait up, Kid," Tate said. "I'll come with you."

The Kid put a hand on the old lawman's shoulder as Tate started to get up. "Sorry, Marshal, but you have to stay here."

"But I don't want to."

"It'll be fine. Your daughter will take good care of you."

"I won't let you run off again and scare us half to death, that's for sure," Bertha snapped.

Tate shook his head. "I . . . I don't understand . . ."

"There's a big surprise." Bertha stood up and strode across the room to take hold of her father's arm. "Come with me. I'll take you to your room. And you'll stay there this time, do you understand that?" She glanced at The Kid and added in a clearly dismissive tone, "Thanks again."

"Sure." The Kid stepped back and got out of the way as Bertha helped her father to his feet and urged him out of the parlor and down a hall.

"You can let yourself out," she called over her shoulder to The Kid.

He stepped out onto the porch and eased the door closed behind him. From inside the house he heard Bertha saying something else to Tate, and although he couldn't make out the words, the angry, hectoring tone was clear enough.

Going down those steps and walking back to his horse was one of the hardest things The Kid had ever done. *Yeah, that bunch of outlaws would be welcome right now,* he thought. *You could even throw in an Apache war party.*

Just about anything would be better than this.

273

Chapter 30

He was still worried he'd done the wrong thing by leaving Tate at his daughter's when someone knocked on the door of his hotel room that evening. He wasn't expecting any trouble, but habit put a gun in his hand anyway as he went to answer the summons.

When The Kid opened the door he found a man he had never seen before standing in the corridor. The man wore a brown tweed suit and had a mustache, bushy side whiskers, and a harried look about him. He didn't seem threatening.

"Mr. Morgan?"

"That's right," The Kid replied. "What can I do for you?"

"My name is Timothy Edwards. My father-in-law is Jared Tate."

"Of course," The Kid said with a nod. "How do you do, Mr. Edwards?"

"Not too well right now. Have you seen Jared?"

The Kid shook his head. "Not since leaving him with your wife at your house this afternoon. Isn't he there?"

"No, the old—" Whatever Edwards was about to say, he stopped himself and took a deep breath. "He's run away again. My wife claims she was watching him the whole time, but some-how he got out of the house and disappeared."

"Have you gone to the police? He couldn't have gotten far."

"Well . . . he took his horse with him. Bertha searched the neighborhood, but by then he was long gone."

The Kid realized he was about to smile and managed not to. He was sort of pleased Tate had lit a shuck out of there, but some legitimate reasons to worry about him wandering around by himself came to mind.

"We thought maybe he might have come here, since the two of you seem to be friends," Edwards went on.

"We rode some tough trails together, that's true. But I haven't seen him. He wouldn't have known where I was staying, anyway."

"No, I guess not." Edwards chewed worriedly at his drooping mustache. "I'll have to go to the law. They'll find him, and when they do, I'm afraid we're not going to have any choice but to . . . to lock him up somehow. We can't have this happening all the time."

"Hold on a minute." The Kid suppressed the surge of anger welling up inside him at the idea of the valiant old lawman being locked up in a little room. "He's got it in his head he still lives in Copperhead Springs. Maybe he headed for there again, like he did before."

"Well, that makes sense. But we still have to find him."

"Of course. I'll start trailing him at first light."

"You really think you can pick up his trail?"

"I know the way to Copperhead Springs from here, and so does Marshal Tate. I can catch up to him. I don't think he would travel through the night. He probably stopped and made camp. He'll be a few miles ahead of me, but it shouldn't take more than a day or two to close that gap."

"But in the meantime something could happen to him," Edwards said. "I don't want my wife put through that."

"You can go to the authorities here, of course. That's probably a good idea. They can search here in town. But I don't think they'll find him. My hunch is he's somewhere out on the trail, like he would have been in the old days."

Wearily, Edwards scrubbed a hand over his face and then sighed. "Thank you. I know this isn't your problem, Mr. Morgan. I can pay you for your help."

"Like I told your wife, just forget about that. Marshal Tate saved my life twice. I'm glad to do anything I can to give him a hand."

"It's funny the way you call him Marshal Tate. He hasn't been a lawman for a long time."

"I reckon Jared Tate will always be a lawman where it counts," The Kid said. "Inside."

• • •

He left at first light in the morning, heading west out of Wichita on the road that would eventually turn into the trail leading to Copperhead Springs. He had no way of knowing for sure that Tate had gone that way, but it certainly seemed likely. The Kid's gut seldom steered him wrong, and it was telling him he would find Tate by going in that direction.

About ten miles west of town he found something supporting his theory. The smell of ashes led him off the road to a small pond where someone had camped the night before. The Kid could see where the traveler had built a fire. He dismounted and hunkered on his heels to study the hoofprints left by the horse that had been picketed nearby. He thought they looked like the prints left by the horse Marshal Tate had been riding for the past few weeks.

The ashes of the campfire were cold. Tate had gotten an early start, too. The Kid swung back up into the saddle and rode on, keeping the buckskin moving at a steady, ground-eating pace.

The first settlers in that part of Kansas had been farmers, and the lack of trees had led them to build their homes out of blocks of sod, usually against the side of a small, rolling hill they had hollowed out. The roofs, which extended out from the hill crest, were of sod and thatch. Those dwellings were cold in the winter, damp always, but not too bad during the summer. As the decades had gone by, the successful farmers had been able to afford to build real houses of lumber, and most of the so-called soddies had been abandoned. Given the materials of which they were constructed, it was no surprise many of them had collapsed, going back to the earth from which they had sprung.

Some of the more sturdily built soddies were still standing, and that afternoon The Kid noticed smoke coming from the chimney of one of them a couple hundred yards north of the trail.

His keen eyes spotted something else, and he reined in. A horse was tied to a hitching post in front of the homestead, and unless The Kid was mistaken, it was the same animal Marshal Tate had been riding.

Tate must have stopped here at this farm, The Kid thought as he swung the buckskin toward the soddy. He hoped they had treated him kindly.

As he came closer and got a better look at the horse, he was certain it belonged to Tate. The chore had turned out to be considerably easier than he'd expected. He could have Tate back in Wichita by nightfall, if they hurried.

A frown creased The Kid's forehead as that thought crossed his mind. Did he really want to take Tate back to his daughter's house? That was what he'd set out to do, of course, when he agreed to accompany the old lawman from Copperhead Springs back to Wichita.

But he had carried out that task, he reminded himself. His responsibility was over. It sure as hell wasn't his job to make Tate stay somewhere he didn't want to stay.

What else was Tate going to do, though? He couldn't be out on his own. Sometimes he couldn't remember even the simplest things. Something was bound to happen to him.

The logic of that realization warred with the revulsion The Kid felt at the idea of Tate spending the rest of his days locked in a room, not understanding where he was or why he was stuck there, never seeing anyone except two people who might as well have been strangers to him. Bertha Edwards might actually love her father, The Kid thought, but she also resented him and had no patience with him.

And he'd never had to walk in her shoes, The Kid reminded himself. He couldn't judge her.

But he didn't know if he could take Tate back to her, either.

With those thoughts racing through his head, he almost didn't notice the fields around the soddy were overgrown, gone back to nature. A plow sat off to one side of the dwelling, but it was covered with rust and obviously hadn't been used for years. The place had been abandoned.

But if that was the case, why was smoke coming from the chimney? Why was Tate's horse tied up outside?

Those questions had just crossed The Kid's mind, causing him to grow wary when a man stepped out of the soddy, pointed a rifle at him, and fired.

The man had rushed his shot, and The Kid heard the bullet pass by his ear with a flat *whap!* He leaned forward in the saddle and drove his heels into the buckskin's flanks to send the horse leaping ahead. At the same time he drew his Colt.

The rifleman worked the gun's lever and fired again, but The Kid charging at him threw off his aim. The slug whined high over The Kid's head. Up close, The Kid recognized the man as the smaller of the two moonshiners he and Tate had encountered on the trail from Copperhead Springs.

"Drop it!" The Kid yelled as he brought up his Colt.

The man didn't heed the warning. He desperately fired again, and a split second later The Kid squeezed off a round. The bullet struck the rifleman and knocked him halfway around, but he managed to stay on his feet.

The Kid left the saddle in a rolling dive that carried him off to the side of the soddy's entrance. The rifleman, swaying from his wound, tried to track him with the barrel of the Winchester. The rifle cracked again and the bullet kicked up dirt uncomfortably close to The Kid's head.

Tilting his gun barrel, The Kid triggered another shot as he scurried to the side of the abandoned building, but the wounded rifleman was already ducking back through the soddy's door. The slug thudded harmlessly into the thick earthen wall.

The man inside couldn't fire at The Kid . . . but he didn't have a shot, either.

"Morgan! Morgan, you hear me?"

The man's voice was thin with strain, and The Kid figured it was from the pain of that bullet wound.

"We got the old marshal in here!" the man went on. "Figured you'd come lookin' for him, and sure enough, you did! Throw your gun away and come out where I can see you, or we'll kill him!"

The Kid didn't say anything. The rifleman had revealed he wasn't alone in there. The Kid figured the man's heavyset partner, the one whose foot the wagon had fallen on, was inside the soddy, too.

"I ain't bluffin', Morgan! You do what I say, or you can listen to the old man squeal while we're killin' him!"

The Kid said, "How do I know he's not dead already?"

The fact that he had responded brought a

crazed laugh from the rifleman. "Take your hand off his mouth and let him talk, Benny."

A moment later, The Kid heard Jared Tate's voice. "Kid, don't pay any attention to what these two polecats say. They're not going to hurt me. They know they'll swing for it if they do."

The marshal's voice was strong and confident. The Kid wasn't particularly surprised. Tate seemed to be at his best in times of trouble, as if he was able to reach down deep in his heart and soul and mind and find the man he used to be.

"You better not listen to him, Morgan," the rifleman warned. "You're the one we really want. Do like I told you, and we'll let the old man live."

The Kid didn't believe that for a second. The men intended to kill both of them.

"You two are lucky goats." The rifleman went on. "I told those gunslingin' brothers where to find you, and I figured they'd kill you for sure. But you come out of that alive, and I hear you beat a whole gang of outlaws, too. Well, your luck's run out, you hear me? Today's the day you . . . the day you die . . ."

The words trailed off into a strangled cough.

The Kid called out, "It sounds more to me like you're the one who's dying, amigo. I hit you pretty hard, didn't I? Think you can hang on long enough to get your revenge?"

"Shut up!" the man yelled. "I'll be fine."

"I don't think so. I think you're losing blood and you're going to pass out soon. Benny's not a killer. I remember that from when we met before. As soon as you're gone, he's going to surrender because he doesn't want to hang."

"Shut up! Benny, I . . . I want you to snap that old man's neck. Wring it like he was a damn chicken!"

The Kid heard the rumble of the other man's voice say, "Selmon, I don't know . . ."

"By God!" Selmon screamed. "Do what I tell you!"

The Kid charged up the side of the hill while Selmon was yelling at his partner. If the soddy had been unused for quite a while, the roof was bound to have been weakened by the elements. The beams were probably rotten. The Kid braced himself for a second, then jumped, coming down as hard as he could near where the stovepipe chimney stuck up through the roof.

Just as he'd hoped, it collapsed underneath him.

The roof crashed down, taking The Kid with it. He slammed into someone as dirt showered around them. His hat protected his eyes from most of the grit, enabling him to see the man called Selmon struggling to get up from under the collapsed roof. Thrusting the rifle at The Kid, he pulled the trigger. Flame erupted from the barrel.

The Kid caught his balance and fired twice.

Selmon's head jerked back as both bullets bored into his forehead and blew the back of his skull off. The Kid wheeled around, searching for Tate and Benny.

Benny loomed up in front of him like a bear, roaring like an enraged grizzly. His hands locked around The Kid's throat as his weight bore the smaller man backward.

The Kid had no other choice. He jammed the Colt's barrel against Benny and pulled the trigger until the hammer fell on an empty chamber. Benny sagged against him, a final breath rattling grotesquely in his throat.

With a grunt of effort, The Kid rolled Benny's corpse off himself and sat up. "Marshal?" He called as he looked around. "Marshal Tate!"

The old lawman pawed dirt off him and struggled to his feet. "Kid, are you all right?"

Relief flooded through The Kid at the sight of Tate, who seemed to be unharmed. He made it to his feet, and pounded Tate on the shoulder. "I'm fine. How about you?"

"Never better . . . now," the marshal answered. "I wasn't sure how that was going to turn out, though. Those boys were loco."

"That they were," The Kid agreed. He checked both men, but just as he'd thought, they were dead. They wouldn't cook up any more moonshine . . . or any brutal revenge plans.

The Kid and Tate made their way out of the

collapsed soddy, leaving the bodies where they had fallen. As they caught their breath, The Kid asked, "Are you ready to go home, Marshal?"

"Back to Copperhead Springs?" Tate asked, his face lighting up.

"No, I'm afraid not. But I've got something else in mind."

Marshal Bob Porter was sitting in a cane-bottomed chair on the porch of his office, smoking his pipe, when The Kid and Tate rode up. Porter stared at them in amazement for a second before he took the pipe from his mouth. "Well, I didn't expect to see you two fellas again so soon."

"It turns out that Marshal Tate needs a place to stay," The Kid said. "From the way you were talking when we were here before, I thought you might have a job for him."

"What about his daughter?"

"I already sent her a wire letting her know that he's safe, and that he'll be looked after. Was I right, Marshal?"

Porter didn't hesitate. He stood up and nodded. "There's a sleeping porch on our house we can turn into an extra room. I can't think of a better reason for doing that."

"Then . . . then I can stay here with you, Marshal?" Tate asked.

"Of course you can," Porter said. "We'll be glad to have you."

The riders dismounted. Tate shook hands with Porter, and the two lawmen slapped each other on the back. Porter suggested Tate go on in the office and he'd join him in a minute.

"Sure," Tate agreed. He lifted a hand. "Be seeing you, Kid."

"*Hasta la vista*, Marshal," The Kid told him with a smile.

When they were alone on the porch, Porter asked The Kid, "Is the law from Wichita going to come after me for kidnapping an old man?"

The Kid shook his head. "I heard back from the marshal's daughter before we ever came here. She wasn't too happy with the idea at first, but she came around. I think maybe she knows he'll be better off here, and she wants what's best for him. She said she can't pay you for looking after him, though."

"Shoot, I don't want any pay," Porter said. "There's still a good man in there. I'll be glad to have him around."

The Kid nodded, but knew he was going to have Claudius Turnbuckle send a regular bank draft to Marshal Porter. Jared Tate would be looked after for the rest of his life, and would be able to spend his days in a place where he was happy and comfortable.

"Where's Holly?" The Kid asked.

"She's at the house. You want to go see her?"

The Kid smiled. "I'm not sure that would be a good idea."

"She'll be mad as a hornet if she finds out you were here and didn't even say hello."

"She'll get over it. Anyway, I've got places to be." The Kid stepped off the porch and swung up onto the buckskin.

Porter followed him off the porch. "Oh? Where's that?"

The Kid nodded toward the west. "Yonder," he said simply.

He waved a hand and was gone, riding out of Chalk Butte, not sure where he was going next but satisfied with knowing he was moving on, answering the call of the frontier while it still existed in the hearts and minds of the men and women who called it home.

Center Point Large Print
600 Brooks Road / PO Box 1
Thorndike, ME 04986-0001 USA

(207) 568-3717

US & Canada:
1 800 929-9108
www.centerpointlargeprint.com